Sherlock Holmes
and the
Adventure of
the American Scalawag

[Being another manuscript
found in the dispatch box of
Dr. John H. Watson, in the vault of
Cox and Co., Charing Cross, London]

As Edited By

Daniel D. Victor, Ph.D.

Book Twelve in the series,
Sherlock Holmes and the American Literati

Hardcover ISBN 978-1-80424-739-6
Paperback ISBN 978-1-80424-740-2
ePub ISBN 978-1-80424-741-9
PDF ISBN 978-1-80424-742-6
Published by MX Publishing
335 Princess Park Manor, Royal Drive,
London, N11 3GX
www.mxpublishing.com

Cover compiled by Awan.

Also by Daniel D. Victor

Cruel September

The Seventh Bullet:
The Further Adventures of Sherlock Holmes

A Study in Synchronicity

Sherlock Holmes and
the Shadows of St Petersburg

The Literary Adventures of Sherlock Holmes,
Volumes 1 and 2

Other Books in the Series
"Sherlock Holmes and the American Literati":

The Final Page of Baker Street
Sherlock Holmes and the Baron of Brede Place
Seventeen Minutes to Baker Street
The Outrage at the Diogenes Club
Sherlock Holmes and the London Particular
The Astounding Murder at Cloverwood House
Sherlock Holmes and the Pandemic of Death
Sherlock Holmes and
the Case of the Fateful Arrow
Sherlock Holmes and a Tale of Greed
Sherlock Holmes
and the Hearthstone Manuscript
Sherlock Holmes
and the Mystery of the Faceless Corpse

3

Acknowledgments

Many thanks to Tom Turley for his critical readings and insightful suggestions. I credit Tom with what works best in the story. Many thanks as well to Judy Grabiner whose close readings, valuable comments, and constant encouragement keep me going. Thanks too to Sandy Cohen who, despite all the challenges that life can throw at one, still finds the time to review my writing. My appreciation to Professor Gary Scharnhorst for providing me with a copy of Julian Hawthorne's parody of a Sherlock Holmes story. In addition, my deepest thanks to my wife, Norma Silverman, who never seems to tire of answering my seemingly endless questions.

A note on the text:
All epigraphs, chapter titles, and footnotes
were added to Dr. Watson's manuscript
by the editor.

A small troglodyte made his appearance here
at ten minutes to six o'clock this morning. . . .
-- Nathaniel Hawthorne (1804-64)
(Author of *The Scarlet Letter)*
On the birth of his son Julian
June 22, 1846

I said to Julian [age 3],
"Let me take off your bib"—
And he taking no notice,
I repeated it two or three times,
each time louder than before.
At last he bellowed—
"Let me take off your Head!"
--Nathaniel Hawthorne
The American Notebook
February 20, 1850

"Good boy! Sharp eyes, and no tongue."
--Henry David Thoreau
On the silent six-year-old Julian
"Studying Nature with Thoreau"
The Memoirs of Julian Hawthorne (1938)

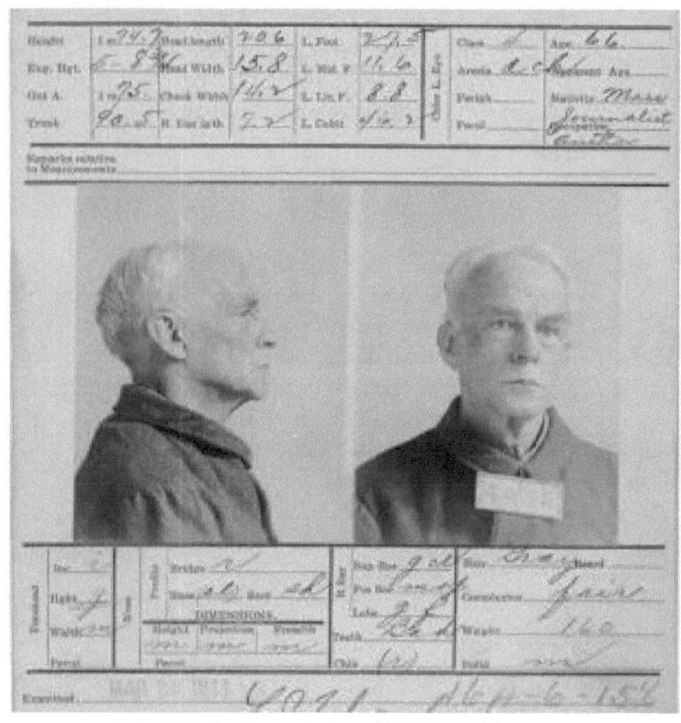

Bertillon Measurement card showing mug shots of
Julian Hawthorne, Inmate No. 4435, at the U.S.
Penitentiary, Atlanta, Georgia, March 26, 1913,
prior to his incarceration for fraud.

Prologue
By
John H. Watson, M.D.

Over the doorway through which we escape
from mortal life, is written DEATH—
an intimidating word at first glance.
--Julian Hawthorne
Shapes that Pass (1928)

Truly, it is not a story that I relish telling. But in order to appreciate fully the significance of the narrative that follows, the dedicated reader must grasp the details of a grisly accident that occurred in the Blackfriars Road during a rain-soaked afternoon in late February of 1878.

For days the terrible tragedy remained a major story in the newspapers, and though I was just then completing the final challenges required for taking the degree of Doctor of Medicine of the University of London, I could not avoid the local newspapers that were saturated with their own perspectives of the collision.

Concerning the most significant of facts all the public prints agreed. A local horse-bus owned by the London General Omnibus Company careened across the sodden Southwark roadway and slammed into a small police four-wheeler headed in the opposite direction. In addition to the driver, the police carriage contained three occupants—a constable, a detective, and a prisoner; and whilst the precise number of passengers riding the 'bus could not be reliably determined, a reporter from *The Daily Telegraph* reckoned that some twenty-three people had been aboard—as many as eighteen occupying the interior and, in spite of the rain, five seated atop on the knifeboard seats.

For some unidentifiable reason—a burst of lightning was suggested by *The Times*—the pair of draught horses pulling the 'bus, a chestnut and a grey, leapt forward. Although the coachman, standing tall in his post and bracing himself at the front of the roof, struggled mightily to rein in the headstrong horses, the large, yellow wheels began to skid, and the 'bus, swerving sideways across the slick road, slammed into the approaching carriage.

Upon impact, both vehicles overturned, and bodies flew about like playthings. Luckily for all the horses, the massive collision caused the yokes and harnesses of both vehicles to snap, and the two teams, suddenly finding themselves unencumbered, bolted in opposite directions, their hoofbeats dissipating in the thrum of the rain.

Long minutes passed before anyone came along to offer aid. Had there been the usual number of pedestrians about, help should surely have arrived more quickly, but owing to the inclement weather—or so reasoned *The Evening Standard*—few people could be found walking the streets. Thus, the bodies that had been ejected from each vehicle, the quick and the dead alike, lay sprawled in the rain among splinters of wood, torn leather-cushions, and 'bus adverts touting soaps, theatre tickets, and furniture polish.

When witnesses did eventually summon doctors and the police, the *Standard* opined that the injured turned out to be the lucky ones, for the authorities reported that the frightful collision had resulted in the deaths of seven passengers from the 'bus and of all four from the carriage belonging to the Metropolitan Police.

Generally speaking, I have found that people may be forgiven—even encouraged—for neglecting to recall the terrible accidents that do not involve an individual they know or—worse still—a loved one. Yet in that brutal meeting of the twain, the omnibus and the four-wheeler, in Blackfriars Road, there developed a fatal irony so memorable that it continues to render the collision difficult for even the most casual of observers to put out of mind.

Crucial to the mordancy was the ultimate destination of the police carriage. It was heading for Wandsworth Prison. Having crossed Blackfriars Bridge just minutes before the accident, the four-wheeler was transporting to the site of his upcoming execution a convicted murderer, one Vincent Louder Lovelace, the young artist found guilty of stabbing to death financier Sir Philip Ghent.

To be sure, the collision with the 'bus terminated Lovelace's date with the hangman, yet the convicted killer—still manacled to the dead body of Detective Inspector Reginald Loup—could not avoid his *rendezvous* with justice. Whilst never having to mount the actual steps of the gallows, the murderer of Sir Philip lay dead in Blackfriars Road, the rain unable to wash away the memory of his foul deed.

Or, at least, so believed the people who learned of the story at the time. . . .

J.H.W.
January 1914

Chapter One

The American Visitor

> . . . I mount Mr. H.G. Wells's Time Machine
> and am back in the nineteenth century in a jiffy.
> --Julian Hawthorne
> *Shapes that Pass*

Along with my usual strong coffee that rainy spring morning in 1913, the housekeeper brought me the results from the first post of the day, on this occasion a single envelope bearing an American stamp. Though there appeared no name of its sender on the damp cover, I recognised the cribbed chirography of Sherlock Holmes in the handwritten address, especially in the way he always slanted the *W* in "Watson."

It was little wonder he strove to keep his identity hidden. With political tensions rising throughout Europe, I knew Holmes to be working on behalf of British intelligence. By infiltrating a decidedly anti-British organisation of Irish-Americans somewhere in the States—Chicago, I believed—Holmes hoped to be introduced to actual German spies.

As it turned out, however, the contents of the envelope had nothing to do with Teutonic espionage or even the *Deutsches Heer*. Rather, it was a cutting from *The New York Times* dated a fortnight earlier, the 13th of March, that dealt with the fate of an American writer with whom Holmes and I were both acquainted. In its lead, the article reported that "Julian Hawthorne, son of the novelist who has attained prominence as a writer himself," had been "found guilty yesterday in the Federal District Court of having used the mails to defraud a connection with mines in Canada."

Though Holmes and I were literally an ocean apart, I could still hear him say, "Justice has finally caught up with the scalawag, eh, Watson? Perhaps it is at long last time for you to recount the story of our own involvement with the rascal."

A long time ago indeed—thirty-two years to be precise. Holmes and I had been sharing digs for only a few months when we first met Julian Hawthorne, a meeting that to this day evokes in me the sense of shame responsible for my reluctance to document the story earlier.

Still, I cannot imagine the most critical of readers questioning my hesitation. After all, what amateur detective in his right mind would wish to recall an idealistic intercession that not only undermined an investigation but nearly doomed the lives of two of its major figures? And yet that is the role that I fear I am asked to confront.

For at least two reasons, one remembers Wednesday, the 23rd of March, 1881, with distaste. For the patriotically minded, upon that date the British signed a treaty with the Boers following the British defeat in the war in South Africa. Though military success for England would follow in that part of the world during the years to come, historians like to underscore the fact that the treaty marked the first British defeat since the American Rebellion more than one hundred years previous.

On a less grand scale, the 23rd of March was also the Wednesday that the American writer, Julian Hawthorne, discovered his leather wallet stolen by a skilful pickpocket in the jewellery section of Harrods Department Store. Whilst it was actually not until Thursday that Hawthorne came round to Baker Street to report this indignity, perceptive readers might well anticipate that there was more to the story than simple thievery.

Ignoring our page-boy who was preparing to announce him, the brash American—as yet, still unknown to us—strode boldly into our rooms and commanded our attention. Sporting luxuriant dark hair parted in the middle and a thick moustache that overhung his lips, he appeared a handsome, athletic fellow in his thirties; yet though he was dressed in a fine frock coat and stylish trousers, his cuffs and knees—areas my detective friend has always advised me to observe—clearly showed signs of wear.

"Sherlock Holmes?" he demanded in a deep voice.

My friend stood and nodded.

"My name is Hawthorne," announced the visitor. "I am a writer."

Though much had consumed my attention during the previous few years—medical training, military service, not to mention recuperating from a bout of enteric fever and, more significantly, from the battle wounds I suffered in Afghanistan—I remained familiar enough with the literary scene to recognise so distinguished an American surname.

It was Nathaniel Hawthorne, after all, who had penned such celebrated novels as *The Scarlet Letter* and *The House of the*

Seven Gables. Yet I was also well enough informed to know that Nathaniel had died close to twenty years before, and so I ventured to presume—correctly, as it turned out—that the man who stood before us must have been his son—his only son, I would learn later.

"Julian Hawthorne," he declared and then got directly to the point. "I understand that despite your youth, Holmes, you've made quite the name for yourself in the field of detecting. If such is the case, I have much to discuss with you concerning the fate of the artist, Vincent Louder Lovelace."

Though the horrific collision in Blackfriars Road that claimed Lovelace's life had occurred close to three years before I first met Sherlock Holmes, I clearly remembered the artist's name. I have written elsewhere of Holmes and my early days together—of our initial meeting at Barts in January of '81 and of our subsequent lodgings in Baker Street. More to the point, I have even confessed to the slow evolution of my comprehension of Holmes's profession.

Before discovering that the singular assortment of people who came calling were clients or police, I naively viewed such visitors as "acquaintances." Only later did I learn that my fellow lodger dubbed himself the world's first consulting detective and that the collection of callers were seeking his advice.

In fact, it took Sherlock Holmes some two months after we had first met to include me in one of his investigations. During early March, he received a note from an Inspector Gregson, prompting Holmes to suggest that if I had nothing better to do, I might grab my hat and join him in looking into a murder at No. 3, Lauriston Gardens.

I imagine that it was owing to my successful participation in the case I would later record as *A Study in Scarlet* that Holmes began sharing with me a number of other enquiries with which he had been preoccupied before we met. The Quincy kidnapping and the curious adventure of the butterfly and the milkweed are but two of the early cases he chose to review.

Unlike many of those prior mysteries, however, Holmes had not been contacted by the police regarding the brutal murder of Sir Philip Ghent, the investigation evoked by Hawthorne's mention of Lovelace, Sir Philip's killer.

"The Yarders felt no need to consult me for what they regarded as a simple matter," Holmes explained drily.

Oh, I knew how much my friend disliked being overlooked, and yet at the same time, I also knew how fascinated he remained by the irony surrounding Lovelace's death in the 'bus collision three years before.

"One cannot outrun his destiny, Watson," he enjoyed reminding me.

Thus, I could speak with confidence when I enquired in response to Hawthorne's mention of Lovelace the artist, "You mean Lovelace the murderer?"

Seeming to notice me for the first time, our visitor furrowed his brow. "And you are. . . ?"

"Dr. John Watson," I replied, daring to add just weeks after my participation in the Lauriston Gardens case, "Mr. Holmes's colleague." I extended my hand, but the man had already turned back to Holmes.

"About Lovelace," Hawthorne persisted with typical American brashness. "Let's talk."

"What is it that you wish to discuss?" Holmes asked once we had all taken chairs in our sitting room. "Lovelace admitted that the knife was his, he was found guilty of murdering Sir Philip, and he was sentenced to die. As everyone knows, he was killed in a terrible accident. The authorities were convinced that providence had played the role of executioner, and they closed the case—no questions asked."

Julian Hawthorne smiled mysteriously. This time he addressed us both. "Well, gentlemen," said he, "I for one believe it is well past time to resurrect those questions."

Holmes responded with a smile of his own. "And just why might that be, Mr. Hawthorne? The police were quite satisfied that the matter was closed."

Hawthorne raised his palm as if requesting a pause. "A brief history," said he. "When I first encountered Vincent Lovelace five years ago, he was quite the promising painter. Actually, we met on Leith Hill as members of a hiking group. We both enjoyed trekking about and discovered that other writers and artists met regularly to do so."

"I've heard of the group," I offered, for prior to ever having published a single word, I had been intrigued by the literary world. "'The Sunday Tramps' they're called. Formed by Sir Leslie Stephen, the mountaineer—not to mention editor of *Cornhill* magazine."[1]

"Quite right, Doctor," said Hawthorne, "save the Tramps weren't deemed an official group until '79—at least a year after the 'bus accident. I still go along

---

[1] And father of author Virginia Woolf.

when I have the chance. They get together every other Sunday between October and June."

"Where do they meet?" I asked.

"On the slopes of Box Hill—at the home of George Meredith."

"The novelist?"

"The same. You should join, Doctor. But be forewarned. They go marching all over the countryside. Distances well over twenty miles are not out of the question."

Before my days in Afghanistan, an invitation to surround myself with a group of wordsmiths would have been appealing. But following the wound to my leg that I suffered at Maiwand, I was afraid that such extended trekking days were over.

A sympathetic look from Holmes suggested he knew exactly what I was thinking. In fact, though he appeared uninterested in Hawthorne's prattle, I believe Holmes allowed the American to continue his ramblings in deference to the interest I was showing.

Yet once begun on the topic of his illustrious companions, Hawthorne proved quite difficult to rein in. "I include many prominent artists among my acquaintances," he boasted. "Howard Helmick and Lawrence Alma Tadema, for example. And James Whistler, of course. I didn't care for Jimmie's works at first, but then we became friends, and I discovered that I like his paintings.

"Why, right now, I can picture Jimmie in his studio, his easel and small table that served as a palette to his left, and a charming young woman posed discreetly in front of him. Many's the time I've complimented his work—though I must say," the *roué* added with a lascivious wink, "some of his costumed female subjects might be the more appealing if they were wearing nothing at all. I've told Jimmie so."

The more Hawthorne promoted himself, the more difficult he was to constrain. One need not be a detective to recognise how the cachet of his surname admitted him to the most refined of literary societies. Why, he understood it himself.

Thanks to the fame of his father, Julian had met many celebrated figures, giants he had no hesitation in evoking—fellow Americans like Herman Melville, Ralph Waldo Emerson, and Mark Twain as well as Britishers like Matthew Arnold, Wilkie Collins, Anthony Trollope, and Oscar Wilde. "Literary Bohemia" he called the circle.

What is more, he showed no restraint in passing judgements upon such figures. He remembered Elizabeth Barrett Browning, for instance, as a monstrous tangle of dark hair, and he recalled her son, who dressed in medieval black velvet and silk stockings, as someone worth thrashing.

Despite a few grumblings from Holmes, the garrulous Hawthorne now brought up his childhood. When a young boy in Concord, Massachusetts, Julian would go surveying with the essayist, Henry David Thoreau, and the youthful Hawthorne attended school with the offspring of Emerson and the younger brothers of Henry and William James. Why, he even bragged of a flirtatious romance with an art instructor six years his senior, Abigail Alcott, sister of Louisa May. Julian went so far as to claim to have been the model for the character of the rebellious Laurie in *Little Women,* though Louisa May always denied the charge.[2]

It seemed as if Julian might continue bragging of his noteworthy relationships forever—that is, until Sherlock Holmes had reached his limit. "Enough meandering, Hawthorne," he commanded. "We were speaking of the murderer, Vincent Lovelace; it's beyond time to return to the facts." So

---

[2] According to *Little Women Letters to Laurie* edited by Lis Adams, the portrayal of Laurie was based on two young men—Laddie Wisniewski, whom Louisa May had met in Europe, and Alfred Whitman, who had lived briefly in Concord.

saying, Holmes rose and proceeded to remove one of his commonplace books from a nearby shelf. Thumbing through a number of stiff pages, he arrived at the cutting he sought.

"Allow me," Holmes said and proceeded to read aloud *The Times'* account of the deadly accident presented at the start of this narrative.

"Lovelace is dead," I repeated. "What more need one say?"

Julian Hawthorne patted his moustache. "Have you gentlemen never heard of Edmond Dantès?" he asked.

"Edmond Dantès?" I repeated. "Do you mean that fictional fellow in the novel by Dumas—the prisoner thought to be dead who returns from the grave and becomes the Count of Monte Cristo?"

"The same," smiled Hawthorne.

I remained unimpressed. Ghent's murder was no fiction.

"Well," Hawthorne went on, "suppose I was to tell you that the newspaper report Holmes just read is false—that like the fictional Edmond Dantès, the very real Vincent Lovelace is not dead, that he escaped from England to the Continent, and that he has only just returned from Dresden." Allowing his restrained smile to metamorphose into a broad, all-knowing grin, Hawthorne added, "Oh, yes, one more thing. I should also tell you that, like Dantès, Lovelace too is innocent of the charge levied against him."

"Innocent, you say," observed Sherlock Holmes. "At long last, Watson, a tale worth listening to. Pray, Hawthorne, do tell us all that you know about this matter." As if to emphasise his interest, Holmes picked up his briar and filled it with shag.

"I could tell the story better with a cigar," said our visitor, obviously prompted by Holmes's coddling of his pipe.

In response, I reached for the coal shuttle where we kept our collection of Cuban smokes. I offered a cigar to Hawthorne and took one myself. Once all three of us had lit up, the American leant back in his chair. As if the smoke from the cigar might give him strength, Julian Hawthorne closed his eyes and, breathing in, prepared to begin his narrative.

Chapter Two

The American's Account

Life is inimitable
as well as unsearchable,
omnipresent though it be.
--Julian Hawthorne
Shapes that Pass

Exhaling slowly, Hawthorne removed the cigar from his mouth and bent forward. "Gentlemen," he said quietly, "it pains me to say that my finances are troubling. But we are men of the world who understand such things."

Though understanding nothing, I nodded. Sherlock Holmes puffed sedately on his pipe.

"Flush or not," Hawthorne continued, "yesterday I found myself in need of a pair of cufflinks, and so I dropped into the jewellery department at Harrods." Here he paused to draw on his cigar. "I don't usually have money available for such trinkets, but I had recently sold a couple of book reviews and stories. Perhaps you've seen my writings in the *St. James Gazette* or the *Standard* or

Cornhill. No? Well, they didn't pay me enough anyway. Of course—they never do.

"Still, I decided to indulge myself and had no reservations when the clerk showed me a distinctive silver pair of links with engraved floral patterns. Well, I thought they looked like hawthorn blossoms, and, you know, with the family name, I decided I just had to have them. In fact, I was about to pay when the most surprising of events occurred. I felt a slight tap on my elbow and turned around to see who was seeking my attention. At first, I didn't recognise the fellow—the short hair and the Van Dyke beard threw me off.

"'Julian?' the stranger said, and then I could hardly believe my eyes. Back from the dead had come my old pal, Vincent Lovelace—Vincent Louder Lovelace."

"No," I countered. "You must have been mistaken. As I said before, the man was killed in the collision with the 'bus three years ago."

"So I thought as well, Doctor—at first. Then the stranger actually embraced me. I mean, we hadn't seen each other in years."

"And you're certain it was he?" Holmes asked.

"Not then. In fact, I wanted some time to sort things out, and so I decided to complete the transaction regarding the silver cufflinks. I held up a finger to tell Lovelace to wait and proceeded to reach into my coat pocket for my wallet. That was when I discovered that the damn thing was missing.

"'I've been robbed!' I shouted, and only after the clerk placed the cufflinks back in the display case did he point at Lovelace and say, 'I saw that man put his arms about you. *He* must have taken it."

"'Now see here,' Lovelace exclaimed.

"'I'll get the director,' the clerk advised us, but the commotion already raised brought that very gentleman into our midst.

"'What's going on here?' the newcomer asked and upon hearing the charge, escorted Lovelace and me into a small office not far from the shopping counters."

"Quite a rude reception for someone so recently dead," I observed wryly.

"And it only got worse," said Hawthorne. "By then, I was certain that this stranger was, in fact, my old friend and not someone who would steal from me. I told as much to the director, but since Vincent had been implicated by the clerk, the director wanted to search the accused. Vincent was outraged. Still, he figured that a search might end the matter, so he tore off his coat and hurled it at his two inquisitors."

"One can only assume," said I, "that Lovelace—or whatever the fellow's true identity—was cleared of the crime."

Julian Hawthorne tilted his head to the side. "Not exactly," he said. "You see, inside Vincent's coat the director found my wallet."

I confess to being surprised; Holmes, however, merely emitted a smoke ring that floated upward.

"But here's the strange part, gentlemen. The wallet was empty. I had carried with me enough pound notes to pay for the jewellery. I even had a few greenbacks inside, but all of the money was missing."

"How did the fellow accomplish that?" I asked.

"That's just it, Doctor. I don't think he did. The director was all set to call the police, but I told him that I would not be pressing charges against my old friend."

"How do you explain that he had your wallet then?" I asked.

For his part, Sherlock Holmes was one step ahead of me. Pointing his pipe stem at Hawthorne, he said, "Who else interrupted you?"

"Very good, Holmes," beamed Hawthorne. "I'm impressed. It took me awhile to remember, but there had been a wooden cane leaning against the display case, and just as Vincent approached me, a silver-haired, bearded fellow who said not a word came between us to claim the thing. I had completely forgotten the incident, so shocked was I by the appearance of a figure thought to be long dead, but you were right to anticipate someone else."

"A talented pickpocket," said Holmes. "Adept not only at filching the wallet but also at extracting the money and depositing the wallet in someone else's pocket. And doing it all quickly enough to avoid being observed. The thief made off with the money whilst one of the victims was being accused of the crime."

"Exactly as I interpreted what happened," agreed Hawthorne. "Lovelace himself remembered someone bumping into him. That's when the thief must have dropped off my empty wallet. I couldn't blame Vincent—which is why I chose to keep the police away."

"Where is your friend now?" Holmes asked.

Hawthorne patted his moustache once more. "That is for me to know."

"If the man you encountered really is Vincent Lovelace," Holmes said "if Lovelace is truly alive, then he is an escaped fugitive, and you are guilty of obstructing justice."

"Well," said Hawthorne, "it's a risk I'm willing to take until—if we are to believe that he is Lovelace, which I do—we find out who really killed Sir Philip. To that end, Mr. Holmes, I have come here. Not that either Lovelace or I have much to pay you, but we will offer what we can. I have some extra cash just now." With his right hand, he tugged at the exposed buttoned-end of his left sleeve. "I was unable to buy those cufflinks, you know."

Sherlock Holmes was never afraid of taking a risk, and never more so than in the early stages of his career. "I'll tell you what," he said to Hawthorne, "without giving anything away about this person who claims to be Vincent Lovelace, I'll review with the police the original charges against the man, and then, if I sense there is a new case to be made, you can arrange a meeting between Lovelace, your alleged artist-friend, and Watson and me—that is, Watson, if you're so inclined."

"Dead on," I said, caught up in the spirit of adventure.

"Good," said Holmes. "I'll invite Lestrade for tea and see what we can learn from Scotland Yard."

Before taking his leave, Julian Hawthorne furnished Holmes with his address in the small artists' colony in Bedford Park where he lived with his pregnant wife, Minne, and six children. "We moved there following a disastrous fire in our Twickenham house. Why, Minne had to save the babies from the flames."

One hates to think where Hawthorne might have got himself off to during such a blaze, but at least his family was safe.

"The rent in Bedford Park is quite reasonable," he added with a smile as he exited our sitting room.

Perhaps, it was the "reasonable rent," I thought, *that allowed him the opportunity to purchase fancy cufflinks.*

But once Hawthorne had gone, silver cufflinks were the last items about which Holmes was thinking. "As a rule, Watson," he observed, "detection abhors a vacuum. Another case, and one that presents a new opportunity for getting Sir Philip's murder investigation right—if it was truly mishandled the first-time round. Having witnessed the work of our friends at Scotland Yard before, such an outcome is well within the bounds of possibility."

Chapter Three

The Police Report

Probably our lives are full of symbols
which only an unacknowledged sense perceives.
--Julian Hawthorne
"Absolute Evil" (1918)

Responding to the request of Sherlock Holmes, Inspector Lestrade arrived later that afternoon for tea. Owing to his work with Gregson in the Lauriston Gardens case, I had become familiarised with the pinched facial features of the policeman whose eyes squinted at us from beneath the ubiquitous brown bowler he never seemed to remove. He did not stand very tall, and I believe Lestrade thought the hat gave him added height.

As Holmes had requested, the inspector had brought with him the records from the inquest and trial related to the murder of Sir Philip Ghent. Holding up the papers, Lestrade pulled a face. "Can't for the life of me reckon why you wanted this. The case is—what—three years old?"

"I'm reviewing some prior investigations with Watson," Holmes said—

not exactly the truth, but not far from it. "Teaching him the ways of the consulting detective. As I'm certain you'll agree, Lestrade, every criminal case contains within it the germination of a branch of investigating. The Ghent murder is no different."

Mrs. Hudson brought up the tea along with a plate of chocolate biscuits, and the three of us settled round the table, Lestrade still wearing his hat.

Holmes sampled the tea and then said to the inspector, "If you would be so kind, please inform Dr. Watson what the Yard learned about Ghent's murder."

"Right you are, Mr. Holmes," said the inspector, taking a biscuit, "though as the Americans like to say, the affair was quite clearly 'open-and-shut.' Sir Philip was stabbed to death in his newly built residence in Hampstead. Ghent House, he called it. Though he employed caretakers, a husband and wife, to manage the place, he himself had not as yet moved in.

"On the evening in question, he spent time with a South African business mogul"— here Lestrade checked his notes— "one Jaco van Rooyen. They dined early at Sir Philip's club in Pall Mall, the Pericles, where Sir Philip had temporary rooms. Van Rooyen left about seven o'clock, and Sir Philip decided to pay a visit to his new home. As work neared on the house's completion, he would frequently stop in to see how matters were coming along. Though it was a five-mile walk from the Pericles to Hampstead, Sir Philip was in the mood for exercise."

Lestrade paused to savour a biscuit, and as he ate, he took the opportunity once again to look over the pages he had brought with him.

I too nabbed a biscuit before the inspector resumed his summary.

"The housekeeper, a Mrs. Charles, admitted Sir Philip to his new home some time about nine. He told her to send up any guests who might come to see him because anyone who did show up that late would probably be coming for business reasons."

Lestrade consulted his notes again. "Ah, yes," he said, pointing to a line in the handwritten text. "Sir Phillip also said something to Mrs. Charles about an appointment he had arranged. But he said that he himself would attend to the French windows in the dining-room that served as a side entrance to the house. He also told her eager he was to spend the night in his new home for the very first time. According to the housekeeper, it was with a sense of excitement that Sir Philip proceeded to the library.

"One half-hour later, Mrs. Charles responded to a knock on the outer door. Vincent Lovelace was seeking Sir Philip; in his hand was a foot-long, cylindrical package wrapped in paper. We know now that it was a Japanese knife with a carved handle." Lestrade handed Holmes a drawing of the weapon.

"Difficult to tell from a drawing," said Holmes as he looked closely at the paper, "but the handle is no doubt ox-bone, and the tapered blade, about six inches long, is probably a *Sakai*—extremely sharp and constructed like a sword."

"What was Lovelace doing at the house in the first place?" I asked.

"Ah, yes," said Lestrade, tilting upward the brim of his bowler. "The motive. For that, we must go back in time."

"Quite so," observed Holmes, "the starting point of many a crime."

"For the motive," said Lestrade, "we have the traditional love-triangle. Sir Philip had married in his youth, but his wife died, and they'd had no children. At the same time, he was the guardian of a distant cousin, a lovely young woman named Mercédès Perle. Her father, Alain Perle, who was French, died when she was quite young, and Sir Philip came to the rescue of both her and her mother. In fact, he cultivated so strong an interest in the young girl that he took responsibility for her general upbringing. He paid for her education and, as she grew older, invited her to all the right social gatherings."

"Quite the generous fellow," I said, thinking all the while how Mercédès also happened to be the name of Edmond Dantè's love in *The Count of Monte Cristo,* the novel already referred to by Julian Hawthorne. What is more, I would eventually discover that the young lady's appellation was spelled with the same French accent marks that appear in Dumas' book.

Lestrade waved his forefinger at me. "Don't be so sure of Sir Philip's generosity, Doctor," said he. "The man had a nasty reputation among the business classes. But for Mercédès and her mother, he went so far as to set aside a small trust fund that allowed the pair to live in a comfortable flat in Chelsea. As Sir Philip's financial resources increased, he decided to build a large home in Hampstead, and it seemed obvious to him that such a place required a new wife to go with it. Mercédès came to mind."

"Twice her age, was he?" I asked.

"At least," answered Lestrade. "What's more, during the trial the young lady described how she regarded her cousin more as a friend than a guardian. The mention of husband never came up. Still, his fiftieth birthday was approaching, and Mercédès, who had done some painting, thought that a portrait of herself might be a fitting gift. At a dinner-party, she had recently met Lovelace and, sharing an interest in art, asked him to paint her."

"Ah, yes," said Holmes, leaning back in his chair and steepling his fingers. "The eternal triangle."

"As I said," agreed Lestrade smugly, as if the so-called triangle could resolve most extreme aspects of human behaviour. "And why not? Lovelace was a tall, handsome, long-haired fellow. Walked about beneath a cape and a wide-brimmed hat. Quite the bohemian, don't you know? Attractive to a young lady, at any rate."

"I wouldn't offer a guess," said I.

"At the same time, Lovelace was charmed by the sitter's beauty. What is more, during the weeks it took him to complete the portrait, he also came to know her winning nature. Despite the continual presence of the young woman's mother, he fell in love with his model."

"A modern-day Pygmalion," I said.

"Pygmalion?" Lestrade repeated. "Don't know the bloke."

"A Greek," said Holmes. "Not to worry; nothing to do with the matter at hand."

Lestrade shrugged. "In any case," he said, "before asking her to marry him, Lovelace decided to obtain official approval—not from her pliant mother since he knew that she would go along with whatever Mercédès wanted. Rather, he decided to ask the proper person in authority, her guardian, Sir Philip Ghent. To acquire his permission was what put Lovelace in Sir Philip's library that fateful night."

"Let me guess," I offered. "Sir Philip said no."

"Righto, Doctor, at least, as Lovelace told the story. That was when Sir Philip announced he wanted the young lady all for himself. Sir Philip, you see, planned to ask Mercédès for her hand. It was all quite unexpected."

"But if Lovelace was simply going to ask Sir Philip a question," I wondered aloud, "why did he bring along a knife?"

"Excellent point," Holmes said.

"Oh," smiled Lestrade superciliously, "Lovelace had an answer. He had no problem admitting that the Japanese knife was his. He said that because he knew Mercédès especially admired the carved handle, he planned on giving the knife to her later that night as a betrothal gift once Sir Philip had granted Lovelace permission to propose to her."

"But things didn't go as planned," I observed.

"Right again, Doctor. Lovelace claimed that he was so upset by Sir Philip's refusal, that Lovelace stormed out of the house and—if you can believe this— said he forgot to take the knife with him. The prosecution believed neither his reason for bringing the knife to Ghent House—'silly,' Queen's Counsel called it—nor his explanation for leaving it there. The prosecutor argued that the murder was premeditated and that Lovelace brought the knife to Ghent House with the intent of doing harm."

"Unprovoked, do you mean?" I asked.

"Who knows?" answered Lestrade. "Lovelace never said. Perhaps he was going to threaten Sir Philip to get his approval."

"Strange way to begin a marriage," I said. "Any other suspects? What about whoever Sir Philip had told to come in by the side entrance?"

Lestrade shook his head. "No one saw such a figure—if there even was one. Oh, Mrs. Charles, the housekeeper, said there might have been a bearded chap talking with Sir Philip in the shadows of the library late that night, but we paid her no mind. She hadn't put on her spectacles, she said. On the one hand, she believed it might have been Lovelace she saw, but on the other she thought the fellow had a higher-pitched voice than Lovelace's. In the end, she practically admitted she couldn't be sure of anything going on in there."

Holmes displayed a sceptical smile.

"Be that as it may," Lestrade went on, "the next morning Mercédès, accompanied by her mother, arrived at Lovelace's studio in Soho to pick up the portrait for her guardian. According to Mrs. Perle, 'Lovelace looked a wreck—maybe even sick or drunk.'

"Lovelace told Mercédès he wouldn't part with the portrait. He would keep it for himself. He told Mercédès that Sir Philip intended to marry her, and she said that, though she cared for her guardian, she could never marry him. In fact, Mercédès confessed to Lovelace that, during the last few weeks of sitting for her portrait, she had fallen in love with him.

"Upon hearing those words, gentlemen, Lovelace actually admitted that he was so angry at being denied by Sir Philip that he said—" at this point, Lestrade bit into another biscuit and once again consulted the pages before him. We had to wait until he finished the morsel to hear the exact wording from the police report.

"Lovelace was so angry at Sir Philip," Lestrade repeated, "that he shouted"—here the inspector read the quotation directly from the page, "'I could have killed the man.'"

"Most conclusive," I said.

"Wait, Doctor," said Lestrade, "there's more. An hour or so before the drama in Soho took place, Mr. Charles, the caretaker at Ghent House, was making his early-morning rounds and saw the door to the library ajar and the gas lamp still on. A moment later, he discovered Sir Philip's body lying face-down on the library floor, the Japanese knife with its carved white handle sticking out from his back. The blade had penetrated the left lung and pierced the heart; the small rug upon which the body lay was soaked in blood.

"Mr. Charles sent for the police, and the first constable who arrived found—in addition to the body, of course—the safe open and some papers inside. When I got there and surveyed the scene, however, I found nothing of significance in the safe."

"What was it that you deemed not significant?" Holmes asked.

"If you must know," Lestrade sighed, "it was a hand-written murder mystery based on a case of one of my colleagues. A piece of fiction. No title-page; no author listed. Nothing to get worked up about."

Holmes cocked an eyebrow in response. "Which colleague?"

Lestrade took a deep breath. "Gregson," he muttered.

The policeman's reticence was understandable. To discover a story based on the success of his rival did not ease the friction between himself and Gregson that we had encountered in the Lauriston Gardens matter.

I wondered what else had been discovered. "No money in the safe?" I asked.

"Not that we know of," said Lestrade.

"How did you settle on Lovelace then?" I wanted to know.

"Once Mrs. Charles told us Lovelace had visited Sir Philip the night before, Inspector Loup went to the artist's studio to question him."

"Loup was the detective subsequently killed in the 'bus accident if I remember correctly," I said.

Lestrade nodded. "Poor fellow. In any case, he arrived just in time to hear Lovelace inform Miss Perle—as I've already told you—that Lovelace was angry enough to have killed Sir Philip himself. When Lovelace admitted to Loup that the knife was his—well, Loup was a smart fellow. That was enough for him to hear. He arrested Lovelace for the murder."

"I should think so," I said. "His guilt was a foregone conclusion."

"Right you are, Doctor. To confirm the point, Lovelace was found guilty at the trial."

I nodded my approval.

"And yet," said Lestrade, "the proceedings were not without additional interest."

"How so?" asked Holmes.

"A woman called Fiona Plumb showed up at the Old Bailey and announced that, unknown to anyone, she was actually Sir Philip's widow. Much closer in age to Sir Philip than was Miss Perle, she said that they had been married the previous year in the States but that Sir Philip wanted to keep the news quiet until they could make the announcement in the new house in Hampstead."

"You say no one knew about this?" Holmes asked.

"No, but before you make any of your deductions, Mr. Holmes, let me reassure you. We found their marriage certificate in a search of Sir Philip's desk in his rooms at his club."

"If that was the case," I wondered, "then why did Sir Philip say he planned to marry Mercédès Perle?"

"Another excellent question, Watson," said Holmes. "You show promise."

I felt my face redden at the compliment.

"Nothing to do with Sir Philip's death," Lestrade said with a note of finality. "In fact, following the inquest and trial, Lovelace was convicted of the murder, and—since the jury believed that bringing the knife indicated premeditation—the judge donned the black cap and sentenced him to death."

"Quite final, that," I said. "Were there no mitigating circumstances in Lovelace's favour?"

Lestrade pulled down the brim of his bowler and crossed his arms in front of his chest. "The man was guilty," intoned the policeman. "No more need be said."

Holmes leant forward. "On the contrary, Lestrade. Your adamant expression of certitude suggests that there must have been something else, a counter argument."

"Well," the policeman muttered, "I suppose there's a bit more that can be said. Though it has nothing to do with the murder."

A cocked eyebrow revealed Holmes scepticism.

"Not long after the newly revealed wife—that is, she who is now Lady Ghent—moved into Ghent House, she sacked both Mr. and Mrs. Charles, the caretaker and the housekeeper. Mr. Charles has since died, and his missus currently lives with her sister in Dulwich."

Sherlock Holmes clenched his jaw. I could sense his frustration. After Lestrade had left—the policeman did manage to collect another biscuit before making his exit—Holmes asked, "What do you think of someone coming in through the side entrance, through those French windows that Sir Philip mentioned to his housekeeper?"

"If they were unlocked," I said, "why then anyone could have come into the house unseen.'"

"Quite so—anyone—including the bearded man Mrs. Charles may or may not have seen in the library."

Novice though I was, it nonetheless seemed clear to me that there was more to be learned about the night of the murder than we had just heard from the police inspector. Equally clear, as Sherlock Holmes so frequently liked to remind me, a representative of Scotland Yard would not be the most reliable source from whom to get the answers.

Chapter Four

A Meeting with the Dead

Memories are one thing,
and the facts on which
they were begotten are another.
--Julian Hawthorne
Shapes that Pass

The letter that arrived in the evening post from Julian Hawthorne confirmed what both Sherlock Holmes and I had surmised— Vincent Louder Lovelace was eager to meet with Holmes. The recently resurrected artist did, however, issue a caveat: In no way would he agree to come to the centre of London again.

Lovelace had already returned there once in his search for Hawthorne, but after having been accused of stealing his friend's money at Harrods, Lovelace insisted that he wanted to maintain greater separation between himself and the headquarters of the Metropolitan police, a constabulary most definitely interested in re-capturing an escaped prisoner long-thought dead.

Yet Hawthorne expressed no desire in hosting such a meeting at his home. Even though Lovelace was staying with Julian's family—Hawthorne's wife Minne and their six children—in the Chiswick suburb called Bedford Park, Julian clearly wanted to shield his family not only from any knowledge of Lovelace's notorious reputation, but also from his own complicity in sheltering a convicted murderer.

On the other hand, Bedford Park, being a goodly distance from Scotland Yard, made an ideal location to meet with a fugitive from the law. I myself, having done some advisory work at the Chiswick and Turnham Green Dispensary, knew the area. To this day, in fact, it is a quiet community filled with red-brick, multi-gabled houses, many a roadway lined with trees like plane or cherry, and inhabited by not a few artists and writers. Remaining in the general locality seemed an intelligent plan, and we agreed to meet mid-morning at a neighbourhood public house.

As Hawthorne would later inform us, the Tabard in Bath Road stood less than a mile from his own home in Woodstock Road. Like most of the other structures in Bedford Park, the many-gabled, terraced block of three buildings that included the pub was of relatively recent construction. Yet with its projecting bays, Chaucerian name, and pebbled plaster and red-brick facade, it was obviously intended to evoke the romanticised grandeur of taverns and inns from prior centuries.

Two columns frame the portal and, passing beneath the sign that depicts a horn-blowing herald draped in the eponymous tabard, Holmes and I walked through the tiled entry and into the whitewashed taproom. At a rear table far from the small-paned windows at our backs were seated Hawthorne, who acknowledged us with a nod, and his friend, Lovelace.

My literary agent, Arthur Conan Doyle (not yet *Sir* Arthur) whose interest in the spirit world has been well-documented, would have been disappointed. But Vincent Lovelace appeared most corporeal indeed. Clearly no venturer from the Other Side, the artist presented himself not as some cape-wearing, long-haired, bohemian wraith, but rather—as Hawthorne had described him at Harrods—a neatly-bearded, closely cropped fellow in conventional dark jacket and white-linen shirt.

Both Lovelace and Hawthorne sat with a Guinness in hand. It seemed a bit early for alcohol, but since the two men were drinking, Holmes and I made our way to the wood-panelled counter and ordered the same.

When we returned to the table with our drinks, Hawthorne pointed upward. "You know," he said, "this place has seven gables. Like the house in my father's novel—a good omen."

Lovelace in turn offered a toast. Holding up his tankard, he proclaimed, "To clearing my name."

"Hear, hear," said Hawthorne, and he raised his own drink in support.

Holmes cocked an eyebrow, but we both joined in.

"It is clear to me," Holmes said to Lovelace, "that you escaped from the police during the chaos in Blackfriars Road three years ago."

Hawthorne was about to sip his ale, but at Holmes's observation he exploded with a derisive hoot. "Quite the detective," said he sarcastically.

Lovelace raised both his hands. "Please, Julian," he pleaded, "Mr. Holmes is here to help me."

"One presumes," Holmes continued, "that the collision in the Blackfriars Road killed your police captors. Since you were still manacled to Inspector Loup, you must have secured the key from his pocket and freed yourself. One imagines that in the turmoil of the accident, you discovered a nearby corpse of your size, but—luckily for you—with a face badly disfigured in the accident. You donned the unfortunate fellow's coat, and handcuffing the body to Loup allowed you to make your escape"

(The astute reader, who questions why fingerprints would not reveal the false identity of the corpse, should be reminded that the common use of such marks was still more than a decade away.)

"Why," marvelled Lovelace, "it's as if you were there, Mr. Holmes."

Holmes waggled his long fingers to imply, "It was nothing," but I had already learned how much he enjoyed such compliments.

"Save, of course," said Lovelace, "that you neglected to describe the horrors. Twisted bodies dead and alive. Groans and screams. Smears of blood. As an artist, I will forever remember the terrible tableau."

Holmes's account reminded me of Dumas again, but in the wake of Lovelace's gruesome description, we all sat silently by, not even moving to take a drink. Laughter at another table eventually broke the spell, and I dared bring up *The Count of Monte Cristo*.

"When Lovelace put on the dead man's coat," I said to Hawthorne, "he imitated Edmond Dantès again. Remember how Dantès managed his escape in the shroud of a dead prisoner from the island prison—"

"Chateau d'If," Hawthorne, the *Monte Cristo* enthusiast, reminded me with a wry smile.

"You may be able to escape from the law," he murmured between sips of his Guinness, "but you can never escape Dumas."

Lovelace returned us to reality. "Fortunately," he said, "if such a term can be applied to so terrible an accident, I found money in the pocket of the jacket I'd removed from the corpse. It was of no use to the dead man, I reasoned, and so I felt no guilt in keeping it. All that was left was to stagger to my feet and grope my way out of the awful mess.

"'Are you all right, sir?' I recall someone asking. I don't know who it was. I just waved him off and managed to get to a train station. The dead man's money enabled me to take the train to Julian's house."

"Seven miles," Hawthorne said. "We lived in Twickenham then. I've already told you about the fire that caused us to move."

"This is Lovelace's story," Holmes reminded the American. "Allow *him* to furnish the details."

"I don't remember the details," Lovelace grimaced. "All I know is that I got on a train in Wandsworth Road and somehow ended up at Twickenham Station."

To no one's surprise, Hawthorne had more to say. Lifting his tankard, as if to celebrate his largesse, he announced, "I didn't have any cash to spare, but I did hide Vincent for the night."

"Weren't you worried?" I said, to the American. "You were helping a convicted murderer make his escape. The law—"

Hawthorne slammed his tankard down on the table. "'The law is a ass,' he said angrily. Then, as if to compose himself, he added, "to quote your Mr. Dickens." Unable to miss another chance to flaunt his connections, he also told us, "Dickens' son Charley, you know, is a friend."

For a long moment, Holmes stared into his Guinness. Then he said, "Pray, continue, Lovelace," his clipped voice revealing his irritation with Hawthorne's tangents.

"Well, as Julian said, I spent the night of the accident at his house. Then early the next morning I made my way to Dover and across the Channel. No one was looking for me. The police reckoned I was dead. Once in France, I trained to Dresden."

"It was my idea, really," interjected Hawthorne. "I studied engineering at the *Realschule* in Dresden a few years before— that was after I was asked to leave Harvard (not enough time for studies while doing sports)—and I told Vincent all about the city."

Lovelace nodded. "It's a beautiful place—in Saxony on the Elbe. But I'm an artist, and what especially appealed to me was its culture—museums, art galleries, and a world-famous opera house."

"All true," Hawthorne confirmed. "And don't forget the wonderful beer and the glorious *Kellers* and breweries to drink it in. I met my wife Minne in Dresden, you know. Don't get me wrong—she's American, but she was living there with her family."

"Sounds charming," I said.

Hawthorne shook his head. "Despite all that, I struggled in Dresden. We thought we'd left high prices back in the States, but anything you wanted to buy turned out to be costly in Germany too. Fortunately, my Aunt Lizzie knew of inexpensive places to live there."

"The Neustadt District you told me," said Lovelace, "so I—"

But Hawthorne had not finished. "At least, I learned enough of the language to get by—no thanks to my father's friend, James Russell Lowell."

"The American poet?" I asked, impressed yet again by the man's lofty acquaintances.

"Who else?" said Hawthorne with a smirk. "The old boy thought that reading *Faust* to me in German would somehow teach me the lingo. No surprise—it didn't. I had to take lessons with a tutor in Dresden, but attending classes while maintaining a family was—as the Germans say—*sehr schwer*. My sons Henry and Jack were both born in Dresden, you know."

"Sounds difficult," I observed.

"Yes, indeed," Hawthorne said. "In fact, a few years ago, I wrote some columns for the *Times* about the challenges of living in Saxony. I suppose I had some rude things to say."

Rudeness from Hawthorne did not surprise me.

"Well, I for one *do* speak German," said Lovelace, "and what's more, I found the community quite open to unknown artists. I gave myself a false name and recruited some students interested in learning to paint. That's where I've been for the past three years, but I've earned enough money to come back here and clear my name. Not to mention seeing Mercédès again."

One had to admire the man's persistence.

Lovelace seemed to sense the same when he asked Holmes, "Do you think I have any chance of proving my innocence?"

"Nowhere is it written that the noblest of intentions produces positive results," said Holmes. "Yet I do believe there is some reason for hope."

"Like what?" asked Hawthorne.

In answer, Holmes raised his forefinger. "First, there are the questions surrounding Sir Philip's marital status. Fiona Plumb profited most from his death."

"It was she," I pointed out, "who inherited Sir Philip's money and new house."

"Indeed," said Holmes. "And yet there was no mention of Mercédès Perle or her mother in the will even though Sir Philip had been supporting the pair for years."

"None," said Lovelace.

"And yet, if in fact Sir Philip really had secretly married Fiona Plumb in America, why would he tell *you* that he was intending to marry Mercédès Perle?"

"That's the question, isn't it, Mr. Holmes?" said Lovelace. "What's more, no one else seemed to know of this marriage; we only learned of it from Fiona Plumb herself."

"Fortunate for her," I said, "that the police found the will and marriage certificate at Sir Philip's club."

"Strange and suspicious," mused Holmes.

"To tell the truth," said Hawthorne looking askance, "it has always sounded a bit *too* suspicious. Smells like some kind of underhanded deal on Fiona Plumb's part."

The American—or so it seemed to me—possessed a degree of expertise in underhanded matters.

"What else do you see in my favour, Mr. Holmes?" Lovelace asked.

"Well, we plan to speak with the *maître d* at Sir Philip's club, the Pericles, and—"

"The people who work at those places can be helpful," Hawthorne interrupted. "I'm a member of the Savage Club, and they—"

"Yes, thank you, Hawthorne," Holmes replied coldly.

"I went to the Pericles on the night of the murder," said Lovelace. "I was looking for Sir Philip to ask for Mercédès' hand. I gave my name to the doorman."

"Did you now?" said Holmes. "Such behaviour also speaks to your innocence. People planning to do murders don't generally go about identifying themselves in advance."

"I gave my name to the housekeeper in Hampstead as well," said Lovelace eagerly. "That should count in my favour too."

Holmes nodded.

"And don't forget," I put in, "that we know from the police report of other people besides yourself who might have been at Ghent House the night of the murder."

"A fellow with a beard, wasn't it?" said Hawthorne. "The housekeeper mentioned him at Vincent's trial."

"That's right," I said, "though apparently the police dismissed the idea. And there was also the possibility of someone entering through a French window."

"No doubt the same fellow," said Hawthorne quickly.

"They might indeed be the same," observed Holmes.

"Most certainly, they are," the American repeated, sounding strangely certain.

"Yes, Hawthorne," said Holmes sharply, "but they might also be different. In either case, the police showed no interest in either one since the case against Lovelace was so strong."

The artist put both hands round his tankard. "Will you pursue this then, Mr. Holmes? You sound like you see the possibility of helping me." He raised the tankard towards Holmes. "It's the first real hope I've had in years."

Though Sherlock Holmes returned Lovelace's gaze, he did not raise his own drink in response. "I believe in justice, Lovelace," said my friend simply. "If the pursuit of justice frees you, so be it. But if the pursuit of justice confirms your guilt, you will find Scotland Yard rapping on your door at my personal behest."

"I welcome the challenge," proclaimed the artist.

"To justice then," said Julian Hawthorne eyeing each of us in turn, and we all raised our glasses in reply to his toast.

Chapter Five

What the Porter Had to Say

Nature seems to welcome
defiance of conventions,
and to say with a smile,
"So, the truant has come back again!"
--Julian Hawthorne
"Absolute Evil"

The Pericles Club stands at the west end of Pall Mall. It is not far from where Mycroft Holmes, my friend's brother, would eventually rent rooms and later still, across the road, would help found the Diogenes Club, whose primary rule of silence Mycroft could enjoy without having far to travel from his digs. I knew none of this whilst visiting the Pericles, of course, but then it would also be a few more years before I even learned my friend had a brother.

In particular, the Pericles welcomes members of the financial district. Whilst some of the most prestigious clubs in London feature relatively modest entry-ways— Boodles and the Reform Club come to mind—the Pericles is not among them. One cannot miss its street entrance: Beneath a broad fanlight, oaken double-doors stand between a pair of tall, sentry-like, potted ferns which themselves appear dwarfed by the stately Ionic columns directly behind them. A smartly dressed doorman in frock coat and silk top hat completes the scene.

It was just such a grey-haired figure who touched his brim to us later that same day as we alighted from our hansom under a bright spring sun. "Good afternoon," said he with a professional smile, the smile I was certain he used for anyone who might possibly have reason to enter the club.

Though he looked us over from head to toe, a mere glance at our casual clothing would have been sufficient to inform him that we were not members. "Haven't seen you here before," said he. "Wot's your business?"

"I am Sherlock Holmes," my friend announced, "and I am a private detective. I would like to speak to someone in authority regarding a murdered Pericles member a few years ago."

The smile faded from the doorman's lips. "Sir Philip Ghent, I should imagine you're referring to. Ask inside for Mr. Atwater, the major-domo. It was to him the police spoke about the matter." The doorman leant forward as if to speak in confidence. "It was from here at the Pericles that Sir Philip left just before he met his death, you know."

"Quite," said Holmes. "And your name is?"

"Wilkins. Just Wilkins." Then, with the caveat not to trouble any of the club members, he opened the right-hand outer door and motioned us inside.

"Thanks very much, Wilkins," I added, hurrying to keep up with Holmes who had already entered the building.

In dramatic contrast with the daylight outside, darkness shrouded the foyer. The small area was illuminated by candles set upon a narrow, stand-up desk, which guarded the archway leading into the Pericles' grand hall. A trio of paintings that featured race horses in varied poses hung upon the left-hand wall, and heavy drapes covered the right.

Posed behind the desk was a gentleman in formal dress who, upon our arrival, had been perusing some pages in a ledger, probably a list of the evening's guests. When we entered, he looked up to see who was disturbing his universe.

One glance at Holmes and me reassured Mr. Atwater—for the personage was indeed the man to whom Wilkins had referred us—that he had no need to greet us with even a smile that would fade. In fact, he agreed to speak about Sir Philip's murder only after Holmes threatened to question the club's members when they departed the building.

"Yes," he was indeed working on that fateful night when Sir Philip was killed. "Terrible business," he offered, but had nothing more to add than what he had told the police. "Sir Philip seemed in excellent spirits; he planned to spend the night in his new house in Hampstead. Beyond that, I can add nothing."

"The search of his rooms?" Holmes prodded.

Mr. Atwater frowned. "Oh, yes. The police found some papers, Sir Philip's will and his marriage licence as I recall." Following those words, he resumed whatever he was doing with the ledger. It was clear he had nothing more to say to us.

Once we had exited, Holmes turned back towards the doorman. "Did the police talk to you about that night, Wilkins?"

"No, sir, they did not. As far as I could tell from the newspapers and the talk round here, they had their man in custody and didn't need any additional tittle-tattle."

"To what sort of tittle-tattle are you referring?"

"Well," Wilkins shrugged, "as I heard it told from one wot works inside, Sir Philip had a bit of a row with a South African gentleman—Mr. Jaco van Rooyen. Hard to remember all the facts, but I recall him in particular because of the walking stick he carried—black ebony it was, with a small silver skull for a handle."

"Quite distinctive," I said.

"Aye, but hard to understand him. Mr. van Rooyen speaks with a thick accent. Sounds German. Some say he was seeking money from Sir Philip to finance a diamond mine—maybe after our defeat out there, Mr. van Rooyen felt he deserved British money. But Sir Philip, he wanted no part of it. Accused the man of exploiting the natives. Or some argument along those lines."

I could understand that it was not the sort of argument an authority like Mr. Atwater would want representing the Pericles.

"The misunderstanding about the diamond mine didn't seem to bother Sir Philip much," Wilkins said. "He was planning to go to his new house in Hampstead. Had someone to meet there. Told me so himself when I offered to call him a cab. 'No, Wilkins,' he said, 'it's a nice night for a walk. It'll help me forget the argument I just had.' He reckoned it would take him about two hours to get there, but he seemed eager for the exercise and set off.

"Minutes later, Mr. van Rooyen came out. He was still angry from his argument with Sir Philip and asked me if that '*skurk* Ghent'—his words, not mine—had left. I pointed the direction Sir Philip took. Mr. van Rooyen had me hail a hansom, and he climbed in and told the cabbie to drive in the direction I'd indicated."

"That could be significant," I mused aloud.

"I know it's been years now," said Holmes to Wilkins, "but is there any chance you can remember the cabbie?"

Wilkins smiled. "In fact, I do recall the cabbie; he's a mate. Frequents Pall Mall nightly. Sometimes we're off work together and share a pint. Loomis is his name. You can pick him out by his elegant horse. Calls him Cooper, he does; the beauty has a diamond-shaped blaze on his face with a snip at his nose.

"Wot's more," said Wilkins, lowering his voice, "though I can't be certain, I believe that I saw someone else—a small fellow—not Mr. van Rooyen—maybe with a beard though it was too dark to see for sure—set out after Sir Philip. Now it could have been a coincidence, but he come out from behind the shadows of that building over there"—Wilkins pointed across the road—"at the same time Sir Philip began his walk."

Again, a foggy reference to someone with a beard.

"As I said, could be just a coincidence, but this fellow turned off the road at the same place Sir Philip did. It looked to me like the bloke *might* have been following him. Mind you, I said, '*might*.' But I can tell you this: If Sir Philip really was followed that night, it certainly wasn't by the man they said wot killed him. The artist-fellow came a half hour later—like I said. Gave me his name, he did. 'Loveless,' I recall."

"Love-*lace*," I corrected him.

"Yeh, wot I said. I remember the fellow. Not every day some *artiste* with long hair and a cape comes round with a package that looks like it could be a cricket bat or a machete or—dare I say?—even a long knife. He was looking for Sir Philip. I told him Sir Philip went off to his new house in Hampstead."

"You didn't tell this to the police?" I questioned.

"Never asked old Wilkins about Sir Philip, did they?"

"I'm glad *I* was the one who did," said Holmes. "Thank you very much indeed."

Wilkins touched the brim of his tall hat in quiet response, then signalled for a hansom. The cab arrived within minutes, and before we climbed in, Holmes handed the doorman a couple of coins along with a small card containing our Baker Street address. "Send your friend Loomis to see me," said Holmes. "Tell him there's a few pounds to be earned for his trouble."

Holmes was silent for most of the drive home, content to stare out at the passing buildings. But as we headed up Baker Street, he turned towards me. "In the forenoon tomorrow, I intend to pay a visit to Mrs. Charles, the housekeeper who now lives in Dulwich. Afterwards, I shall stop in at Ghent House itself and meet Sir Philip's widow. I think there is much that may be learned from both women. You're more than welcome to join me, Watson."

"Of course, I'll join you, Holmes," I said quickly. I had not as yet secured a regular medical position, and in fact I could not imagine a more exciting way to spend the day.

Chapter Six

Two Ladies

Women of all ages will play with death.
    --Julian Hawthorne
    "Absolute Evil"

The next day, Saturday, Holmes and I visited Mrs. Imogen Charles, the former housekeeper at Ghent House. From information furnished by Lestrade, we learned that Mrs. Charles now toiled as a seamstress in Dulwich where she lived with her sister Maud. Maud was employed as a servant at Dulwich College, and her husband worked as a porter there. The two of them shared a small cottage not far from the school on a leafy street off the Alleyn Road.

(It would be close to fifteen years before another case would bring Holmes and me back to Dulwich—though the reader may be forgiven for not recognising the institution in the sketch I titled "The Adventure of the Three Students." To preserve the distinguished reputation of the school, I did my best to conceal its identity. Still, Holmes's success in the enquiry indirectly resulted in introducing us to the student called Raymond Chandler whose exploits I recounted in the 1903 investigation called *The Final Page of Baker Street.* As it turned out, Young Chandler worked as a boy-in-buttons for Mrs. Hudson at 221B and went on to become a published poet and essayist.)[3]

But I digress.

On the particular Saturday in question, we found the house whose address Lestrade had provided. Mrs. Imogen Charles, a stout, bespectacled woman with grey hair, put aside the frock she was mending and quite frankly appeared all too eager to discuss the final days of her previous employment.

"Sir Philip was a pleasure to work for," she told us. "Sidney—Sidney was my late husband—Sidney and I used to bless our

---

[3] Watson did not live long enough to learn of Chandler's mystery novels like *The Big Sleep* and *The Long Good-Bye*, both based on experiences Chandler shared with Sherlock Holmes and chronicled by Watson himself in the aforementioned *The Final Page of Baker Street.*

lucky stars to have found such positions. Oh, I know that business people found him rough, but he was always helping others, Sir Philip was. Kind to young Mercédès and her mum, wasn't he? Terrible shock to Sidney and me when Sir Philip died so tragically. Can't have the same kind words for that woman he married in America, can I? Though I must say that Sidney and I knew nothing about any such union. Wouldn't have believed it if they hadn't found that paper in Sir Philip's club."

"The marriage certificate, do you mean?" asked Holmes, "The one the police discovered in Sir Philip's desk?"

"The very same. America. Who knew Sir Philip was married there? Wasn't told he'd even been there, was I? Must have been while the house in Hampstead was being built. Weeks would go by between his visits. At first, Sidney and I lived in the lodge near the front gate. We moved into the house itself only after the construction was completed. We were delighted when Sir Philip stopped by. Planned to spend the night for the first time, he said."

"Ah, yes," said Holmes. "That final night. I understand that you admitted Mr. Lovelace that evening."

Mrs. Charles furrowed her brow. "He seemed like a nice fellow. Gave me his name when I asked."

Just as Lovelace said, I remembered. *He offered his name to Wilkins outside the Pericles and then again to Mrs. Charles at Ghent House.*

"Most eager to talk with Sir Philip," Mrs. Charles went on. "Mind you, I saw the package he carried. Not that I knew it was a knife; it was all wrapped up. Three years later, and I still can't believe what happened."

Sherlock Holmes leant forward. "You said at the trial that Lovelace was the only visitor you or your husband let in to the house that night."

"Yes, that's true."

"But what about the man with the beard you saw in the library."

"Neither Sidney nor me let him in, did we? And the police, they weren't interested in hearing about anyone else. I suspected that they had the one what done it. Sidney told me not to make trouble, so after the trial ended, I kept quiet, didn't I?"

Sherlock Holmes's steel-grey eyes shone with intensity. It was a look that I came to recognise whenever a new clue seemed imminent.

"What was it you would have told them had you not kept quiet, Mrs. Charles?" Holmes asked.

"Well, I would have told them more about the other person Sir Philip expected later that night, the one he'd told to come round the side-entrance, the one Sir Philip said he'd let in himself."

"What more do you have to say about him?" asked Holmes. "Did such a person really come?"

"I can't be certain, but various times whilst I was falling asleep, I believe I heard voices and people moving about."

"One person? Two?" Holmes queried. "Might a voice have been accented?"

I assumed he was referring to the South African.

"I can't be certain," Mrs. Charles repeated, "save to say that sometime past one I woke up. I remember thinking I might have left a candle burning in the hallway near the library. So, I get out of bed, put on my night-dress, and walk out into the corridor. That was when I saw a light in the library and heard people talking. It seemed a long time for Mr. Lovelace to still be there, but then I never saw him leave and thought it was probably him in the room with Sir Philip."

"But," Holmes persisted, "you're suggesting it might also have been someone else?"

"I'm wondering if it might be whoever Sir Philip had let in at the side-entrance. I'm curious by nature, you see. So,

I blow out the candle I found still burning in the corridor and take a quick glance inside the library."

"And what did you see?" Holmes asked quickly.

"First, I should say that when I got out of bed, I didn't put on my spectacles. Didn't need them, did I? I knew the way. But I'll be honest with you, Mr. Holmes, I can't see too clearly without them, and the door was open only a crack."

"Yes?" prodded Holmes.

"Well, the police think I saw Sir Philip talking with Mr. Lovelace. But I know they were wrong. Oh, Mr. Lovelace might have been out-of-sight elsewhere in the room, but the fellow I saw leaning over the desk was smaller. Though it might have been the shadows, I think he may also have had a beard. I said so in court. But here's the thing, Mr. Holmes—"

"Yes?" my friend said, his voice ringing with expectation

"This man's voice was higher pitched than the voice I thought I heard earlier. I believe there might have been another stranger in there as well."

Sherlock Holmes clapped his hands together in delight. "One can read the details of a trial," said he, "but it's so much more vital to hear what happened from the witnesses themselves. Was the person you think you saw tall, thin, fat?"

"Couldn't say for certain, but not too large, like I already told you. Sidney didn't want me talking about any of this since I was so unsure. Why, he wouldn't even want me talking to you right now. But it doesn't really matter anymore. Sir Philip is dead."

"Quite so," said Holmes.

"Then that woman moved in—Lady Ghent as she now calls herself—and our lives were rearranged. She wanted us out, no questions asked. I believe it was the thought of relocating that killed Sidney. Bad heart, don't you know? We asked for some extra time before going, but she told us to leave immediately. Sidney took ill when we were packing up and died within days.

"I was just fortunate that my sister was willing to take me in. Maud and her man have been very good to me. You know, the new wife at Ghent House didn't replace us. I heard from the cook at a house nearby. No staff at all, just a housekeeper who comes in once a week to clean, and then there's a cook. And there's that man who does her every bidding."

"Man? What man?" Holmes asked.

"Too smooth a bloke, if you ask me. Roland Wattle is the toady's name—waits on her hand and foot."

Holmes stood up, and I followed. "You've been most helpful, Mrs. Charles."

"Indeed, most helpful," I reiterated rather lamely.

"Come, Watson," said Holmes, "time to return to Baker Street."

Holmes was fairly bursting with energy as we walked towards the West Dulwich train station. "Additional suspects, Watson," he pointed out to me. "There's Roland Wattle, who gained quite the position as a result of Lady Ghent's rise. There's the mysterious caller at the French window, and perhaps the bearded chap Mrs. Charles thinks she saw in the library. At the very least, we have a few new threads to pull, threads about which the police—as is their custom—apparently never gave a thought."

Holmes was quiet on the train during our return to London. In retrospect, I realise he was already contemplating our visit to Hampstead later that day.

Rattling along the Ring Road, a hansom conveyed us from Baker Street, round Regent's Park, and into Hampstead. A few turnings beyond the shops and restaurants in the High Street and we were heading in the direction of the expansive East Heath.

Immediately thereafter, we passed the foreboding walls and mansard roof of Appledore Towers, the shadowy abode of the notorious blackmailer, Charles Augustus Milverton. At the time, of course, we had no knowledge of the malefactor and thus no way of predicting that in a number of years not only would Holmes and I be burglarising that very house but also witnessing the unspeakable crime that would take place there.

Another turning put the Towers behind us, and almost immediately we were driving up a brief incline and coming to a halt before a black, wrought-iron gate that interrupted a six-foot brick wall. The gate was open.

"Ghent House, guvnor," the coachman shouted down.

"Continue," responded Holmes.

The hansom lurched forward, and passing through the gateway, we proceeded along a semi-circular, gravelled drive to the entrance of the house itself, a modest two-storey villa of white-washed brick. It was not nearly as large as the mansions in the neighbourhood, but I still found it hard to imagine living in such a place without the help of an adequate staff. Yet according to Mrs. Charles, that was exactly the case.

We dismissed the cab and approached the outer door, bright crimson in colour and adorned with a brass ring and lion's head for a knocker. It was a young man who answered Holmes's rapping, presumably the Roland Wattle about whom Mrs. Charles had spoken. He was dressed informally in a suit of brown corduroy, his brilliantined brown hair dramatically combed straight back.

"Yes?" he enquired.

"I am Sherlock Holmes," said my friend as if the name of the young detective should be enough to gain entrance.

"Yes?" the fellow said again. "We don't have time to talk with every gadabout who comes to the door. Police, reporters, busybodies. . . ."

"I am a private detective," Holmes said and pointing in my direction, added, "this is my associate, Dr. John Watson."

The man snorted. "Should take money from you lot. Might as well set up a tollbooth right here. The booths on the Albert Bridge aren't used anymore. Could place one just by the door and collect money from gawkers like you."

"We would like to see Lady Ghent," Holmes stated.

The fellow smiled condescendingly, as if to question how foolish could we possibly be. "I'm afraid she is engaged at the moment," he said. "Perhaps you can leave your card, so she may contact you if she is so inclined once she learns what the matter is about." He tilted his head as if to elicit from Holmes the nature of our call.

"Tell Lady Ghent," Holmes said coldly, "that I have questions to ask related to the murder of her husband."

The young man seemed to stand straighter and examined us with keener scrutiny. "Why, that was years ago! It's old history, I'm afraid. Lady Ghent misses Sir Philip, but has nothing new to say on the manner of his passing."

"Well," said Holmes, "convey to her that *I* have something to say on the matter of his passing. We look forward to her response."

The fellow shrugged in agreement, but rather than inviting us inside to await Lady Ghent's answer, he shut the door and let us cool our heels upon the front porch. As the door closed, the ring on the knocker banged on its own, seeming to underscore our exclusion.

Minutes later, however, the fellow reappeared and ushered us into a sitting room, a chamber accoutred with ornate brass fixtures and overstuffed furniture. From garish paintings to floral-patterned pillows, riotous colours fought with one another for dominance. One could not imagine a more convincing scene to epitomise the appetites of the *nouveau riche*.

The gentleman indicated we be seated, and Holmes and I settled into the deep cushions of a red damask couch whilst he sat upon a mauve wing chair that faced us. For some small time, we suffered through an awkward silence, but finally the rustle of a gown announced the appearance of the mistress of Ghent House, and all three of us rose to greet her.

Lady Ghent, the former Fiona Plumb, was a petite, blonde woman of approximately forty years. Attired in a green satin dress that left her shoulders exposed, the handsome Lady Ghent appeared the flame that attracts the moth—or so it seemed she aspired to be.

"Mr. Holmes, Dr. Watson," said the lady, extending a dainty hand first to Holmes and then to me.

"A pleasure," I responded.

For his part, Holmes remained silent.

"Please, do sit down," said Lady Ghent, indicating the damask couch from which we had just arisen. She seated herself in the wing chair next to the young man.

"I see you have met Roland," said she with a smile. "We've known each other for years from our work in the theatre."

"Work?" queried Holmes.

"Yes, we both were actors—now retired. We trod the boards, so to speak, at theatres like the Adelphi and the Haymarket. I played the leads, of course. People still talk of my Rosalind in *As You Like It*. Roland was more of a supporting player, and still he remains a great help to me. In the words of Defoe, he is my Man Friday."

Roland blushed but said nothing.

"Now, how may I be of service, gentlemen. In addition to giving me your names, Roland said you have some issues you wanted to discuss related to the passing of my husband."

"Quite so, Madam," Holmes replied. "It has been said that shortly before his untimely death, he had shown an interest in marrying Mercédès Perle. And yet the investigation surrounding his murder revealed him to have already been married at the time. To you."

Lady Ghent allowed herself the briefest of laughs. "Oh, please, Mr. Holmes. That old saw about Mercédès Perle was promulgated by my husband's killer, the miscreant, Vincent Lovelace. No one can take it seriously." Even whilst talking about so delicate an issue, she managed to hold onto the wisp of a smile.

At the same time, I questioned the logic. Whilst it was true that Lovelace might not have known of Sir Philip's marriage, Lady Ghent knew the truth. If as the wife of Sir Philip, she understood there could be no possibility that her husband intended to wed Mercédès Perle, why would she hold on to the idea that so misplaced a sense of rivalry was Lovelace's motivation for killing Philip Ghent? After all, Sir Philip could easily have shared with Lovelace the impossibility of a match with Mercedes.

Holmes too looked sceptical, cocking an eyebrow at Lady Ghent's denial. "No offense intended," said he, "but there was so much at stake in a marriage to Sir Philip. It seems rather incredible to believe Vincent Lovelace would throw about such an accusation if it were specious, especially since it is posited as the catalyst for his alleged impulsive action."

The smile on Lady Ghent's face vanished. From within her dress, she produced a piece of folded paper. "My marriage certificate, gentlemen—retrieved by the police from Philip's desk at the Pericles and given to me after the trial. When Roland told me of your enquiry, I thought it wise to bring it along."

Holmes unfolded the document. It was pink in colour, and he positioned it near enough for me to be able to read its title in bold letters, *Certificate of Marriage, state of New York*. It was dated 17 November, 1877, and it listed Fiona Plumb and Philip Ghent as the bride and groom. The sweeping scrawl of the clerk who had signed his approval was impossible to decipher.

"Well," said Holmes quickly as he handed the paper back to the woman. "This form appears in order and legitimises both your marriage and your claim to Sir Philip's fortune. I'm certain Dr. Watson joins me in congratulating you on your nuptials and, however late, in offering our condolences on the death of your husband."

"Thank you, Mr. Holmes," said Lady Ghent. With a daub at her eye, she added, "It's been three years since his death, and yet I still miss Philip. Your good wishes are much appreciated."

"Thank you," said Holmes. "Dr. Watson and I shall take up no more of your valuable time."

Holmes got to his feet, and I joined him. Lady Ghent also rose, and her man Roland led us to the door.

"Good day, gentlemen," said he with what I can only describe as a smirk. "Don't imagine I'll be seeing the two of you sniffing round here any time soon." He shut the red door with a thud.

Holmes and I walked along the gravelled curve of the drive and then down the hill from the house toward the High Street.

When I was quite sure we were out of hearing-range, I observed, "Your leave-taking seemed rather hasty."

"Quite so, Watson. Once I saw that the marriage certificate was a fraud, I saw no point in staying."

"How do you know it was a fraud, Holmes? It looked legitimate to me."

Sherlock Holmes presented that bumptious smile which suggested how pleased he was with himself. "You wouldn't find it so legitimate," said he, "if you knew as I do that the state of New York didn't begin issuing marriage certificates until last year. Certainly, not in 1877 when Lady Ghent claims she married Sir Philip.

"What is more," he added, "the date was presented in the European fashion with the day written first; in America, it is the month which precedes the day and year. Whoever she hired to forge such a document should refund her money."

One can never pinpoint the sources of Holmes's erudition; one can only marvel at its relevance.

Chapter Seven

A Sunday Afternoon in Chelsea

The truth is that like many other men of
transcendent genius and worth,
my reputation is much sounder
than my bank account.
--Julian Hawthorne
Letter to Robert Carter, Ed.
Appletons' Journal
January 10, 1876

Because Julian Hawthorne had met
Mercédès Perle during one of her sittings for
his friend, the portraiture artist Vincent
Lovelace, Hawthorne seemed a logical
choice to introduce Holmes and me to the
young woman. Thus, following our return
from Ghent House late Saturday afternoon,
my friend telegraphed the American to
confirm the plan.

Once Hawthorne had agreed to join
us in meeting with Miss Perle the next day,
Holmes suggested that I would be a more
suitable questioner than he and that, instead
of joining me and Hawthorne at the interview
with the young woman, he would go off to

Scotland Yard and attend to some matters there.

"You have a way with the ladies, Watson," Holmes said, and I confess that I could not disagree with him.

As far as I could tell in those early days of our companionship, my history of relations with the fair sex certainly overshadowed that of Sherlock Holmes. Still, though I was quite the lady's man before I was slowed down by those Jezail bullets in Afghanistan, even more significant was the comfort I took in the knowledge that Holmes trusted me well enough to handle the delicate interrogation of Miss Perle on my own.

As I slipped into my jacket and donned my bowler that Sunday afternoon, Holmes did make one last request. "When you have completed your interview, be so good as to return here with Hawthorne. I have an issue of some importance to discuss with him. Don't let him say no."

Having learned from Lovelace that Mercédès Perle and her mother lived in a smart flat in Chelsea, Hawthorne agreed to meet me in front of Harrods. Although not on the most direct of perambulatory routes, the department store was easy for my cab driver to find and a logistically convenient location for meeting Hawthorne, thus enabling the two of us to arrive together at Miss Perle's flat.

"Where's Holmes?" Hawthorne asked as soon as he saw me exit the cab on my own. "I thought he was joining us."

When I explained Holmes's reasoning, the American seemed to relish the idea that Holmes deferred to me in the matter of conversing with young women.

"Not as appreciative of the female form as we are, eh, Watson?" Hawthorne queried with a wink.

"Holmes has his methods," I replied stoically.

Hawthorne grinned in response.

Our destination was about a mile away, but it was a crisp spring day, and Hawthorne loved to extol the virtues of hiking.

"Shake a leg, Watson," he exhorted with a clap of his hands. "You'll never get an invitation from Sir Leslie to join the Tramps for a hike if you don't keep moving."

Save for my occasional requests that he slow down, our walk proceeded without incident. Indeed, we maintained a bracing gait along Sloane Street and in less than an hour, near Franklins Row just south of Sloane Square, found ourselves before the small block containing the residence of Mercédès Perle and her mother.

Upon entering the building and climbing the stairs, we located the first-floor flat. With the tug of the bell-pull, Hawthorne announced our arrival, and we were admitted by a woman in tweed whom I took to be the housekeeper.

A single glance about the well-furnished sitting room reassured one that whatever had been the marital designs of the late Sir Philip Ghent towards Mercédès, he had seen to it that his distant cousin and her mother were well-provided for. The Steinway piano nestled within the confines of a broad bay window provided further confirmation.

As elegantly furnished as the room was, however, one's eyes were instantly attracted to the painting above the tiled mantel, the portrait of a beautiful young woman, her proud face framed by tumbles of raven-coloured hair, her piercing brown eyes reflecting interest and concern simultaneously.

Here hung the portrait of Mercédès about which we had heard so much from Lestrade—originally, the proposed birthday gift for Sir Philip whose composition had brought artist and subject together; then, the withdrawn offer; and finally, the lasting symbol of a lost inamorato. Inevitably, Edmond Dantès returned to haunt me, for whilst I gazed at the enchanting portrait of Mercédès Perle, I could not help conjuring an image of the Count of Monte Cristo as he stared at the painting of the Countess de Morceff and recognised in it the vision of his own first love, his own youthful Mercédès lost to him forever.

"It was painted by someone very dear to me," said a mellifluous voice from behind.

I turned and beheld the obvious inspiration for the portrait I had just studied, Miss Mercédès Perle. One could see in her classic visage—the high cheekbones, the strong jawline, the upturned nose—the challenge for an artist to recreate her likeness on canvas. Seeing her attired as she was—in a form-fitting, reddish-purple dress fringed with lace and ruffled in white near the hem—one could also understand why an artist like Lovelace undertook the challenge and why the completed work would have proved a fitting birthday gift for her now-deceased guardian.

"I will never give up Vincent's painting," she added. "It is all I have left of him."

So striking was the corporeal appearance of the portrait's subject that one scarcely noted her mother, the ageing, grey-haired woman dressed in dark-blue who had accompanied her daughter into the room. For propriety's sake, the mother would remain present throughout our conversation.

Though a married man, Julian Hawthorne seemed to come alive upon the arrival of Mercédès Perle. No sooner had she come into the room that with a broad smile, he moved towards her and kissed her hand. To his credit, he paid his respects to her mother as well and introduced me to both of them.

"Would you care for tea, gentlemen?" Mercédès asked.

Hawthorne seemed ready to accept, but I intervened. "Thank you for your kind offer, Miss Perle, but we are here as part of a new investigation into the death of Sir Philip Ghent and will forego the social graces."

"Upon arranging our meeting here today," she replied, "Mr. Hawthorne alerted me to the nature of your visit." She indicated that we should all sit down, and once we did, it took her but a moment to address the controversy of the relationship between her guardian and herself. "Let me say from the start, gentlemen, that Sir Philip was a kind and generous man, but I tell you frankly that

I could never consider marrying someone thirty years my senior even though he was so fabulously wealthy."

In spite of himself, Hawthorne let out a snort. "I can only wish that my wife Minne had the kind of money Sir Philip did. I'd marry her all over again."

Mercédès Perle confirmed all of what Inspector Lestrade had reported. In early '78, she had hired Lovelace to paint a portrait that she planned to give as a birthday gift to Sir Philip. Quite openly, she admitted that during the course of numerous modelling sessions, she fell in love with the artist.

"I tell you truthfully, gentlemen," she said softly, "were Vincent—that is, Mr. Lovelace—alive today, I would be his wife."

If I am any judge of sensitivity, such a truth seemed readily apparent.

"Following Sir Philip's death," she went on, her hands clasped tightly in her lap, "I could not believe the charge of murder levelled at Vincent—at Mr. Lovelace. I was distraught over his conviction, the death sentence that accompanied it, and the frightful ride in the police carriage that rainy day in Blackfriars Road. If you must know, Doctor, it's been three years, and I am still distraught. The courts may reach whatever decisions they wish, but I don't for a moment hold Vincent responsible for Sir Philip's murder."

Her mother shook her head, an obvious though silent rebuke of what she interpreted to be her daughter's naïve blindness.

If Lovelace were as innocent of the murder as the young woman believed, then another perpetrator was required. Sir Philip had been stabbed in the back. There was no struggle involved, and a woman could be quite as capable of wielding the blade as any man.

Although I had every intention of phrasing my question as delicately as I could, I felt compelled to ask, "Is it not possible, Miss Perle, that unlike most other people involved in this case, you had some knowledge of Sir Philip's already-existing wife and that knowledge hardened you against him?"

For her part, the young woman displayed no hesitation in responding directly. "Are you suggesting, Dr. Watson, that I might have been irate enough to have killed him myself?"

"No, no," I said, immediately embarrassed by her inference. Rather foolishly, I thought my question to have been more hypothetical. Not only was Mercédès Perle quick to speak her mind, I realised, but equally quick to discern connections. Still, her response did lead me to another question. "Do you have any strong feelings today towards Lady Ghent?"

She offered a quick smile. "Are you wondering if I might be envious—perhaps, even angry with Lady Ghent—because Sir Philip had made *her* his wife instead of me?" She shook her head. "It is true that according to his final will, my mother and I will no longer be recipients of Ghent largess. In fact, though I have been offering painting and piano lessons for the past two years—" here she pointed at the Steinway—"we'll soon have to move. Still, I hold no grudges. One cannot forget Sir Philip's original kindness."

Sweeping her arm round the room to underscore her point, she said, "Look at all that he provided. I wished for Sir Philip only the best of fortune and happiness—and certainly, the opportunity to marry whoever might have struck his fancy."

"Besides yourself, of course," Hawthorne pointed out needlessly.

"Yes," she replied.

Prompted, perhaps, by the simplicity of her answer, Hawthorne proceeded to ask what turned out to be the most personal question of the afternoon. "It's none of my business," he said, "but I'd like to know if you have found some other man who holds your interest?"

"No," Mercédès Perle responded with a blush. "For me, no one can replace, Mr. Lovelace."

Her mother shook her head once more, and it seemed as good a cue for us to take our leave as any other.

"Obviously, she still loves him," Hawthorne beamed as we exited the building. "The law be damned; we have to bring the two back together. I must give the news to Lovelace."

So enthused was he that he was about to take his leave. But I grabbed him by the arm as I recalled Holmes's request.

"A moment, Hawthorne," I said. "Actually, more than a moment. Sherlock Holmes would like to speak with you. He wants you to return with me to Baker Street."

A furrow darkened the man's brow. "Why, Baker Street is in the opposite direction from Bedford Park."

"Holmes was really quite insistent," I said. "Pretend you're trekking with your literary friends in the Tramps."

Hawthorne stroked his thick moustache as he considered his decision. "Well," he said at last, "if you're willing to walk, I guess I'll join you."

With a degree of trepidation, I forsook the comfort of a cab, and we set off in the direction from which we had come. Before we reached the first turning, however, I noted a bent-woman in black dress and bonnet involved in a discussion with a constable concerning directions to one of the nearby bridges.

I thought nothing of it at the time, yet as we crossed various streets and approached the greenswards of Hyde Park, I caught sight of the same woman trekking along behind us, and my suspicions grew. Perhaps the detecting skills of my fellow lodger were inspiring me, but I wondered if we were being followed.

I mentioned as much to Hawthorne, and his reaction was immediate. Rather than pretending to be unaware of our pursuer and surreptitiously monitoring her behaviour, he stopped short on the gravelled footpath, turned round, and flexed his not inconsiderate musculature.

"Where is this fellow?" he demanded.

"Not a fellow," I told him, "but a woman."

Hawthorne grinned at what I imagine he believed to be the absurdity of such a situation—some young woman fast on his trail. The grin faded, however, when I described the ageing, stooped figure of our pursuer. Worse, there was no one in sight resembling such a woman.

A few more paces along the footpath brought us within sight of the serene waters of the Serpentine, the man-made lake in Hyde Park, and of the ancient oaks in the background reflected on its surface. On this occasion, however, it was not the mirror-lake that caught my attention; it was a wooden bench nearby, for sitting upon it was the very woman in black whom I thought had been following us.

Immediately, I stopped and indicated her presence to Hawthorne. He took the lead, and the two of us approached the bench. In an instant, however, Hawthorne and I were both taken aback. Peering at us from beneath the black bonnet were a familiar pair of steel-grey eyes.

"Holmes!" I cried out in disbelief.

Hawthorne was speechless.

"What is the meaning of this?" I asked.

Sherlock Holmes remained seated. Though he maintained his feminine posturing, he spoke softly in his usual voice.

"In this investigation," said he, "we've learned of someone following Sir Philip from his club on the night he was killed. And then there was the thief at Harrods who must have been following Lovelace—"

"And stole my money," Hawthorne reminded us.

"If Miss Perle is somehow connected to Sir Philip's death, I thought it more than possible that your meeting with her might attract additional scrutiny. So that I could observe in disguise is the primary reason I decided not to join the visit."

Though one assumes that Holmes could not discern my hurt feelings, I realised that I had been too hasty in thinking he regarded me as an accomplished detective. He had sent me off to ask questions of Mercédès Perle so he could be free to scrutinise whoever might be following Hawthorne and me.

The American interrupted my self-pity with the proper question. "And did it?" he asked. "Did our visit attract scrutiny from somebody?"

"Perhaps," said Holmes. "There was a grey-haired fellow with a cane who trailed you for a bit."

"The South African at the Pericles had a stick," I said.

"So did the pickpocket in Harrods who filched my wallet," Hawthorne reminded us.

"Well, Hawthorne," replied Holmes testily, "I can't be certain who it was because, whoever he was, he disappeared when you did your dramatic about-turn."

"I make no apologies," said the American. "I just did what came naturally."

Holmes refrained from further comment on the subject. "Let's return to Baker Street, shall we, gentlemen?" Holmes said. To the American in particular, he added, "I have a few questions I would prefer to raise in the privacy of our rooms. I'm sure Watson told you of my intention."

Hawthorne nodded. "He did, Holmes, though I can't imagine whatever you have to ask will justify how far out of my way you have taken me."

"Let's see, shall we?" said Holmes. Then he rose from the bench, but to conceal his height kept the crook in his posture. "I'll accompany you back to our rooms, gentlemen," said he, "but I suggest we find a four-wheeler. I've spent too much time already bent over in this get-up."

Begrudgingly, Hawthorne grunted his acquiescence, and I hailed a carriage.

Holmes remained in character when the growler arrived, and maintained it when we alighted in Baker Street.

After we passed through the outer door at 221 and were about to mount the stairs, Mrs. Hudson, our landlady, came to see who had entered. Holmes's female appearance did not fool her. In fact, it elicited nothing more than raised eyebrows even when he requested from her a quick meal of roast beef sandwiches. Unlike myself, it seemed that Mrs. Hudson was getting used to the eccentricities of her new boarder.

"So, Holmes," said Hawthorne, as soon as we had passed into the sitting room, "I've come quite a distance. Just what is the important subject you need to talk to me about?"

Holmes removed his bonnet and dark wig. "Right to the point, I see," he said. "Well, let's talk about the night of the murder in Ghent House. Though the police have not recognised the relevance of the fact, it is time to examine a bit of evidence I have uncovered. It is why I wanted to speak with you today."

"What is that, Holmes?" queried the American. "Something meaningful, I hope."

"You be the judge," said Holmes. "I had already learned from Inspector Lestrade of the handwritten story about his colleague that had been found among the items in Sir Philip's open safe on the night of his murder. I already knew its author was unlisted. Upon further enquiry, however, Lestrade informed me of the story's title, which appeared on the first page—'A Mystery from the Notebook of Inspector Tobias Gregson.'"

At Holmes's recitation of the words, Hawthorne patted his moustache.

"Although a piece about a fellow Yarder did not seem to interest Inspector Lestrade, it interested me—especially, since I already had formed my suspicions. And so, this afternoon, when you two gentlemen were meeting at Harrods in preparation for your walk to see Mercédès Perle, I took the opportunity to visit Gregson at the Yard before coming to Chelsea myself.

"The inspector was most happy to talk with me, and together we examined the story that had resided in Sir Philips' safe, an investigation about a woman drowned in a bathtub whose details Gregson told me he'd shared with you."

"Yes?" said the American.

"I think you can tell me what I learned about that case, Hawthorne. But I also believe you have much more significant information to impart."

I could only wonder to what Holmes was referring.

"Hawthorne, what were you doing at Ghent House on the night of Sir Philip's murder?"

The American's face paled, and the man who usually appeared quite in control of his emotions now seemed decidedly ill at ease. There would be no explanation forthcoming, however, for Hawthorne, clearly unnerved at Holmes's revelation, sputtered, "Not—not much to say, really," and stormed out of our flat.

I looked to Holmes for clarification.

"It's all quite simple, really. Gregson told me he'd spoken with Hawthorne about the drowning case. Moreover, whilst no author's name appears on the manuscript, the handwriting is consistent with Hawthorne's penmanship in the letter we received from him concerning our meeting at the Tabard. What he was doing at Ghent House that night and why he hasn't offered an explanation are matters that need to be resolved."

One could just barely hear the slam of the outer door below us, a suitably weak full-stop that punctuated Hawthorne's refusal to justify his appearance at the scene of the crime.

Chapter Eight

Some Answers

*. . . Not often in English history
have more men and women worth knowing
been gathered in London than during
the last quarter of the nineteenth century.*
                              --Julian Hawthorne
                              Shapes that Pass

For the moment, we put the escapades of Julian Hawthorne out of mind. Billy had brought up the roast beef sandwiches prepared by Mrs. Hudson, and no sooner did the page-boy leave than Holmes provided the reason for our hurried meal.

"On a Saturday evening," he explained between bites of well-cooked beef on pumpernickel bread, "the cabs should be canvassing Pall Mall in large numbers. Loomis, the coachman of whom Wilkins spoke, has yet to come here, and we can no longer afford to wait for him to do so."

Holmes poured each of us a glass of water. "If, as I fear," he said after taking a drink, "the fact that Lovelace has returned to England is known, it is only a matter of time before the police come looking for him. We must find Loomis and see if he can shed any light on the mysterious Mr. van Rooyen."

"The South African chap with the silver-skull-topped walking stick," I remembered.

"The same," said Holmes, rising from the table.

"As Wilkins pointed out," said I, "who knows how emboldened such people might feel following the South African victory?"

"Quite so, which is why I suggest we clothe ourselves in the manner of gentlemen. In our search for Loomis, we should appear appropriate surveyors of Pall Mall transportation. Quickly, man."

I managed to scrape together dark jacket and matching trousers, a white shirt and blue tie. For his part, Holmes had exchanged his female dress for formal masculine attire, complete with top hat."

"A far better presentation than your previous costume," observed Mrs. Hudson as we came down the stairs and made our way to the outer door.

Once in Baker Street, we sought a hansom, and within minutes one pulled up in response to our signal.

"Know a colleague called Loomis?" Holmes asked the cabbie before we climbed in. "He's stationed in Pall Mall."

"No, sir," he said. "Not my usual run."

"Well," Holmes replied, "take us there anyway."

We reached Pall Mall in less than half-an-hour and, as we expected, the popular roadway was full of carriages and their high-stepping horses. It seemed easier to walk than to ride, and we exited the cab at the eastern end of the street.

Holmes scrutinised every hansom and horse that passed us, but he also kept a special eye on those standing at the kerb. The Pall Mall toffs usually paid generously for services rendered, and cabbies were constantly seeking affluent patrons in the area. Many a well-heeled swell, having enjoyed the benefits of the numerous gentlemen's clubs lining the street, was more than willing to compensate the coachman who had remained at the ready by the kerb when said-coachman might just as easily have been transporting other paying fares about the city.

Though we both recognised Wilkins positioned in front of the Pericles, on our way to ask him if Loomis was about, Holmes stopped before a hansom parked at the kerb near Waterloo Place. The cab stood just a few paces from the Doric columns that mark the façade of the Atheneum.

"Note the horse, Watson," he said. "Note in particular the diamond blaze and the snip between its nostrils. This must be Cooper, the animal Wilkins described at the Pericles." Following those words, he approached the horse and began to stroke its face and pronounce its name. He spoke loud enough to be heard by the coachman who was sitting up top at the rear of the cab.

"Travelled with me before, have you?" asked the driver.

"No," answered Holmes, "but you come highly recommended by Wilkins, the doorman at the Pericles. Loomis, is it?"

"Right you are, sir," said the man, raising his whip in recognition.

"My name is Holmes," said my friend.

Loomis' bright eyes widened. "You're the gentleman Wilkins told me about. I was fixing to come round to see you. Listening to old Wilkins, there's money to be made talking to you."

Holmes ignored the comment. "Take us round Green Park, Loomis," he replied instead. "And leave the trap open."

"Good as done, Guvnor. Climb right in."

Holmes and I sat down on the padded seat, and when the horse named Cooper started off into the traffic, we fell back against the cushions.

A moment later, Holmes leant back and faced the open trap above his head. "A question, Loomis!" he shouted through the aperture. He had to speak loudly to be heard over the clatter of the horse's hooves. "Do you recall the night of Sir Philip's murder about three years ago?"

"Aye," came the retort from above. "Can't forget it even if I try."

"I believe that a South African called Jaco Van Rooyen was your passenger that night."

"Aye, one of the many."

"And you took him to Hampstead."

Before Loomis answered, he directed the hansom through a few turns on the approach to Constitution Hill. As we travelled up the mild incline, he said, "Yeh, Hampstead. We went to Ghent House, the place where Sir Philip was done in. The gent told me to stop at the gate and wait for him."

"And did you?"

"I did as I was told, didn't I?"

"And what did Van Rooyen do?"

"He went off towards the house. I couldn't see him in the dark. Must have been twenty or thirty minutes I waited."

"Plenty of time to commit the crime," I said softly, "especially with the knife already there."

"What happened when he returned?" asked Holmes.

"He come back muttering something like, 'Too many people mucking about.' Hard to understand him exactly, you know, with his accent and all."

"Anything else?"

"I took him to the Savoy. He paid up and give me some extra. Asked me to come back in the morning and take him to Euston Station for the Liverpool train. He said he was sailing from Liverpool back to South Africa—though he didn't sound or look like an African to me. More like a German or Dutchman."

"And did you return the next morning?"

"I did. He paid well, and I didn't want to miss another chance to earn some more. He'd sent his luggage ahead, so all I had to do was deposit him at the station. He paid me well again and waved me off with his walking stick."

"Anything else, anything else at all that you might remember?"

"His walking stick. It was years ago now, but I still remember the grip of his walking stick. It was a silver skull."

Though Loomis could not see him, Holmes nodded and shouted up, "221B Baker Street, if you please, Loomis." Then he slapped the ceiling, and Loomis closed the trap.

"So," I said, "Van Rooyen went back to South Africa." As we spoke, the darkness of the park was giving way to the winking lights of the city now coming back into view.

"If Loomis is to be believed," said Holmes, "and there is no reason to doubt him. From somewhere in the gardens, Van Rooyen observed too many people coming and going, too many people to continue his argument with Sir Philip or to beg him for more money. No doubt he espied Lovelace and Hawthorne and perhaps even the mysterious bearded fellow whom Mrs. Charles thought she'd seen. Little wonder he decided there was no point in joining the queue."

"If Loomis is to be believed," I repeated, "we can eliminate van Rooyen and rightly count one less murder suspect."

Whilst I pondered the continuing lack of clarity, we entered Baker Street and, upon reaching 221, slowed to a halt. Our trip had not been very long, but Holmes paid Loomis handsomely.

"It doesn't hurt to maintain a generous reputation," Holmes said to me as the cab departed. "Never forget the working class, Watson; they are a source of information that deserve to be cultivated."

As I watched Cooper and Loomis disappear into the night, I appreciated how Holmes was not only nurturing but also investing in the civilian resources so fundamental to his success.

Chapter Nine

The Trembling Lady

Memory and love are parents of art.
                    --Julian Hawthorne
                    Shapes that Pass

At long last we come to the part of the tale to which I rather shamefacedly referred at the start—the meddling for which I was responsible that placed people's lives in danger. And yet I remain certain that the most sympathetic of my readers share the same longing that I did in the moment: the desire to witness the meeting between Miss Mercédès Perle and the lover she presumed dead.

Perhaps, I was prompted by the confidence Holmes recognised in me—my "having a way with the ladies," as he put it. Or, perhaps, like Shakespeare's Friar Laurence who facilitated the meetings of Juliet and her Romeo, I too was inspired by the desire to see the lovers reunited. Even more to the point, Dumas, in fostering his readers' hope for the escaped Edmond Dantès to find Mercédès again, certainly understood that human desire to bring separated lovers together.

Whatever the precise cause and without any presentiment of danger, I took it upon myself to send a telegram to Miss Perle in which I—a person of credibility whom she had previously met—suggested that it would be to her great advantage to take a stroll across the nearby Albert Bridge the following afternoon at two o'clock.

The picturesque bridge—or so I envisioned—would provide a fairy-tale-like backdrop for the romantic reunion I was conjuring. As the bridge was but a fifteen-minute perambulation from her flat in Chelsea and there was the promise of some sort of reward in the end, she responded in the affirmative.

To get Lovelace to agree was an even simpler matter. In spite of our new suspicions concerning Julian Hawthorne and his presence at the scene of Sir Philip's murder, I sent him a telegram in Bedford Park. In it, I informed him that since I expected Miss Perle to be upon the Albert Bridge at two o'clock the next day, he should encourage Lovelace to be there as well and cross from the Battersea side. That way, I knew, the lovers could not miss seeing each other. I closed the message by reminding him not to share the details of the planned meeting with anyone.

Certain that Sherlock Holmes would not approve of my moving the principals of the case about like chess pieces—especially not for love—I too shared the details with no one, in particular, not with him.   Given Holmes's formidable detecting skills, he might have pointed out pitfalls which in my inexperience I would fail to recognise and thereby upset my plan. At the appointed time that Monday, therefore, I simply informed Holmes that I was stepping out to refresh my supply of Arcadia Mixture at Bradley's tobacco shop in Oxford Street and that afterwards I might be tempted to walk about the neighbourhood.

"Really, Watson," said Holmes. "Your leg must be improving.   It's seldom that you volunteer for such exercise."

I shrugged and smiled and left the flat. Moments later I was hailing a hansom for the drive to the Albert Bridge.

I told the coachman to leave me by the steps leading up to the bridge from the footpath on the Battersea embankment, the end-point in whose direction Mercédès Perle would be walking from the Chelsea side.

Since the Battersea location was also to serve as the site of Lovelace's entrance, I hastened up the steps. Immediately, I saw the pair of small, inoperative tollbooths that I remembered Roland Wattle going on about. Ivory in colour, small in size, and octagonal in shape, a pair stand empty at both ends of the bridge. What is more, the nearer one provided me with excellent cover.

From my hiding place, I had a clear view of the Thames. Boats of all natures bobbed along the dark water, the wavelets sparkling in the springtime sun between the two neighbouring bridges, the Battersea to the east and the Chelsea to the west. Moorhens and gulls arced across the pale-blue sky whilst sailors on the passing boats shouted commands, and people on the shore hollered greetings.

As for the Albert Bridge itself—part cable-stayed, part suspension—it features twin pairs of ornate, cast-iron towers standing tall a quarter of the way from each end. Sloping cables and numerous metal stays fan downward from the towers, offering additional strength to support the deck. On this day, the towers' finials caught the sunlight, and some one-hundred feet above the narrow roadway they sparkled like expensive jewels.

As it was a Monday, traffic on the bridge seemed minimal. Children were in school, and sightseers and hikers generally favour weekends for practising their outdoor activities.

Upon Big Ben's stroke of two, Mercédès Perle made her appearance on the footpath at the Chelsea entrance at the far side of the bridge. Readily visible in a simple yellow frock with matching small yellow boater atop her head, she walked slowly forward, scanning the few pedestrians who mingled about her.

I should not have been surprised to discover that Julian Hawthorne had accompanied Lovelace, but as soon as I saw the two of them emerge side-by-side on the walkway not far from where I was concealed, I felt out of sorts.

Yet just as I began to worry that the unpredictable Hawthorne might well interfere in some way with my plan for uniting the lovers, Lovelace espied the beautiful yellow dress and immediately recognised whom it encased. Bolting along the footpath towards Mercédès, the artist left Hawthorne behind to gawp.

Before he reached his beloved, Lovelace must have called her name, for though I could not hear, I had stepped out from behind the tollbooth in time to see the young woman stop and tilt her head. From my vantage point, it appeared that she had no idea who the smartly-dressed man with the short dark hair and van Dyke beard could possibly be.

Lovelace himself came up short when he realised that she did not recognise him. Stopping a few yards away, he gave her the opportunity to look him over and comprehend. It took Mercédès but a moment. With her clear eyes wide, she stared and understood. Her red lips curled into a charming little circle, and she extended her arms wide. Then for everyone to see, the two of them came together and embraced on the footpath of the bridge.

I stood enchanted. For a brief moment, the *affaire de cœur* playing out in front of me appeared in reality all that I had imagined—had hoped—it would be.

Unfortunately, my faithful reader, I must interrupt the very moment of endearment that we have been anticipating together in order to present a relevant note about the eccentricity of the Albert Bridge: When too much traffic or rhythmic stamping disturbs the narrow roadway, the structure has a tendency to vibrate from one end to the other, the reason that over the years, the bridge has earned the nickname, "The Trembling Lady."

Indeed, as the signs posted on the defunct tollbooths still warn the soldiers at the nearby Chelsea barracks:

ALL TROOPS
MUST BREAK STEP
WHEN MARCHING
OVER THIS BRIDGE.[4]

Owing to the sparse traffic that day, there had been no such disturbances, but as I watched the couple, my stance suddenly became unsteady. I sensed an imbalance in the soles of my feet and an awkwardness in the joints of my knees and a churning in the pit of my stomach. In a word, so dizzy did I feel that I had to grab a handrailing for support. I noted that behind me Hawthorne had done the same.

---

[4] Watson is quite right in expressing his concerns about the Albert Bridge. From its opening in 1873, the bridge faced problems with its mechanical resonance and structural integrity. Specifically, the propensity of the bridge to vibrate and shake raised numerous calls for its demolition. Finally, in 1973, two support-piers were added to minimize the issue, and with limits placed on the loads that cross it, the bridge—now painted in pastels and delightfully lit at night—has carried on well into the twenty-first century.

Would that I could blame the enchanting scenario unfolding in front of me for the giddiness I was feeling. But that was not the case. Put simply, the deck of the bridge—its roadway and footpath—had begun to undulate.

The cause was immediately obvious as a large, dark-green four-wheeler came thundering in my direction, the hooves of its pair of black horses pounding rhythmically on the road. With no tell-tale markings to reveal who owned it and manned by a silver-haired driver whose face was almost fully concealed by a plaid scarf, the carriage plunged forward at breakneck speed, people on the footpath frozen in mid-step, mouths agape at the vehicle that hurtled past them; nearby carriages quickly diverting their routes to avoid disaster.

Within seconds, the four-wheeler appeared destined to run down the couple still standing locked in each other's arms. Jumping the kerb as if no step were there, it drove directly at them.

Mirabilis dies! In an instant, Lovelace grabbed Mercédès' hand, and together the two of them dived between an iron stay and the side wall of the bridge behind them. The heavy cable blocked the carriage-driver's foul plan, and immediately the four-wheeler, bouncing back onto the roadway, sped past me, and disappeared somewhere in the curves of the Battersea Embankment.

I hurried as fast as I could to the couple, and though I expected Hawthorne to do the same, the temperamental figure was nowhere to be seen. Still, I ran forward and, recognising the yellow boater in the middle of the roadway, stooped to pick it up.

Lovelace and Miss Perle were brushing themselves off when I reached them.

"Are you all right?" Lovelace was asking her.

The indomitable young woman nodded affirmatively, yet her eyes seemed glazed as I handed her the hat, and she clutched it to her chest.

"That was no accident!" cried Lovelace. "That carriage tried to run us down!"

Mercédès furrowed her brows as if focusing her thoughts. "Who could have been driving it?" she demanded.

"It was as if someone knew just when we would be here," said Lovelace, and he eyed me with suspicion.

"I told no one but Hawthorne," I responded, "not even Holmes. But you know Hawthorne; he likes to talk."

"Julian's my friend!" exclaimed Lovelace. Even as he spoke, he scanned the bridge for the companion with whom he had arrived. Though like me, Lovelace too did not locate him, he would brook no criticism of the man. "Julian would never put Mercédès or me in any danger."

"This attack," I said, "must be related to the murder case we've resurrected."

"Oh, Vincent," cried Mercédès, "if only we can resolve this matter."

Lovelace raised his chin in a heroic pose. "I shall turn myself in," he proclaimed, "and somehow clear my name. And then we shall marry—that is, if you're still willing."

"Oh, yes," she said, "if only we could make it so." And they kissed.

It had been quite a taxing afternoon for all of us, and once Miss Perle straightened her tresses and repositioned the boater at just the right angle, Lovelace took it upon himself to escort her back to her flat. I confess that their betrothal marked the first such engagement I had ever been present to witness.

Not that I had cause to celebrate. For I knew that I had to return to Baker Street to explain to Holmes what had happened as a result of my ill-fated machinations.

Chapter Ten

Hawthorne Explains

Sherlock Holmes always appeared more serious whilst smoking a cigarette. It had to do with the way he narrowed his penetrating eyes when he inhaled. As I stood before him reporting the near-disaster on the Albert Bridge and he sat in his wing chair, addressing me through exhalations of white smoke, his rebuke felt all the more devastating.

"It's quite obvious, is it not, Watson?" he asked, Egyptian cigarette in hand. "The woman was followed, and then the couple was set upon. Recall that I detected a similar situation yesterday upon your return from Chelsea. Why *you* did not infer such a possibility"—here he paused to take a puff—"is far beyond my mind to comprehend."

"Mine too," boldly echoed Hawthorne, who sat facing Holmes. To my surprise, the American had obviously vacated the Albert Bridge in order to rush to Baker Street to inform Holmes of the precarious situation created by my naïve planning. Perhaps, the American hoped that by denouncing my efforts, he might earn a modicum of respect from Holmes following the ill-tempered retreat that ended Hawthorne's previous visit to 221B.

"At least," I said, attempting to vindicate myself, "my idea has produced a positive result."

Holmes cocked an eyebrow at me.

"Lovelace and Miss Perle have declared their love for each other," I reported. "He wants to turn himself into the police, have a new trial, and be freed. Then they can marry."

Hawthorne's scornful laughter reverberated throughout our sitting room. "There is absolutely no evidence to counter the old charges against him," he proclaimed. "Lovelace is a fine fellow, but he's also a dreamer. If he expects to be exonerated, the appearance of another player at Ghent House the night of the murder must be discovered."

The expression on Holmes's face, which had been one of mild amusement during Hawthorne's cachinnation, now turned deadly earnest. "We must talk, Hawthorne," said Holmes. "You must know that."

As if to signal the importance of the next few words, my friend snuffed out his cigarette in the crystal ashtray on a side table. "It is past time for you to explain without prevarication your appearance at Ghent House on the night of Sir Philip's murder."

I for one was shocked by the rapidity of Holmes's change-of-subject.

It was worse for Hawthorne. He had been raucously laughing just moments before, yet now his every lineament seemed to sag as he sat in silent contemplation. At last, following what one must describe as a profound sigh, he murmured, "Yes, I suppose you're right."

With attention no longer focused on myself, I sat down in anticipation of hearing the man's story.

Julian Hawthorne frowned; it seemed clear that he was considering his words carefully. "As I have hinted to you before," he said, "finances have been a problem for me here in England. It's a subject I don't like talking about—money, or lack of it. Would you believe that my father, who you must agree knew a bit about the subject, advised me not to contemplate a career as a writer?"

So typical of Julian, I thought, *to ignore sound advice from so authoritative a source.*

"My family and I settled in Dresden in '72," Hawthorne offered. "But as I've already told you, with prices going up in Germany, the place was becoming like the United States. On the other hand, when I travelled to London to secure the rights for my novels, I was asked to contribute reviews and articles to the *Spectator,* and I discovered that they paid very well.

"So, moving to England seemed to make economic sense. I thought it offered me a promising future. What's more, I've always loved this country. You know, I first came here—to Liverpool, actually—when I was seven, and we stayed for seven years. My father was appointed to the consulship by his old friend, Franklin Pierce."

"The president," I said.

"Yes, they were classmates in college, and my father wrote a political biography for him."

"Nice to have friends in high places," I mused.

Hawthorne smiled wistfully, obviously remembering his father and his own youth.

"To be sure," he went on, "I have fond memories of those days—lots of joy and wonder. But now, since '74 when we moved here, the writers' market has dried up. What a country England is! So much hardship dignified by the majesty of history. Hah! You know, we are thinking of returning to the States as early as this coming fall.[5] I have high hopes for my literary career in New York."

Hawthorne's voice became more animated as he prophesied his future. "You see, I have a connection there with Inspector Thomas Byrnes."

"Byrnes," Holmes repeated. "I know the name. He's the Chief of the Detective Bureau in the New York City Police Department."

"That's the man," Hawthorne nodded. "He was appointed to the position last year, and it was then that I got an idea. I've already told you gentleman about my fascination

---

[5] In *Julian Hawthorne: The Life of a Prodigal Son*, Gary Scharnhorst reports that Julian Hawthorne's family did, in fact, return to the United States in October of 1881. Hawthorne himself, however, traveled first to southern Ireland (allowing him to avoid his English creditors) and then to Belgium, from where, in early March of the following year, he finally sailed home.

with the novel, *The Count of Monte Cristo*. When I learned that Dumas based the book on a true story he found in the Parisian Police Archives, that got me to thinking.

"Why couldn't I do what Dumas did and write a set of fictional mysteries based on some of Byrnes' old cases? It's obvious that people like to read about crimes; creating such stories seemed like a good money-making proposition—it still does."

I know that Holmes and I were in the midst of a serious murder investigation; I had no business pondering my own future in literature. Nonetheless, though my appreciation should probably have gone to Dumas rather than to the man seated before us, I remember contemplating at the time how Hawthorne's promising idea might apply to me.

After all, with a little practise, might I not write an engaging account of my own experiences with Sherlock Holmes? I could begin by dramatising the events concerning the murder in Lauriston Gardens.

In fairness, it is difficult to say that the development of my own authorial career had no other influences. Most important has been the friendship I've cultivated with Conan Doyle, not only my literary agent, but also a celebrated writer himself. If I am being honest, however, I must pay tribute to Julian

Hawthorne as the spark ultimately responsible for *A Study in Scarlet.*

One should not be too hasty, I had come to learn, in dismissing the compositional insights—if not the remunerative aspects of the craft—entertained by the son of Nathaniel Hawthorne. At the very least, the younger Hawthorne planted the seed.

Ironically, it was Julian himself who interrupted my dreams of literary glory. "Before meeting with Byrnes," he explained, "I figured I should get some practice fictionalising a true crime story. All I needed was someone to furnish me the details.

"Back in '78 some of my artist friends had been interviewed by Inspector Tobias Gregson concerning a stolen painting, and they told me he was a bright young man whom I might enjoy talking with."

"Gregson's a good choice," said Holmes, "one of the smartest of the Yarders."

Hawthorne nodded in agreement. "That's just where I found him—at Scotland Yard. I made a proposal to him of dramatising one of his cases. As you know, Holmes, it was the story of a woman murdered—drowned—in her bathtub—and I offered him a percentage of my earnings. He readily agreed and gave me some details. I recorded them in my notebook and converted them into a rough narrative."

"All very interesting, I'm sure," said Holmes, "but how did your meeting with Gregson lead to Sir Philip?"

"Well, I've already admitted to you that money is scarce. I require financial backing to sustain me and my family, and that's especially true during my writing periods. I met Sir Philip at the Pericles and told him about the story Gregson had given me. Unfortunately, it was on the night of his murder that we met."

The night was indeed unfortunate for someone, but I rather doubted it was Sir Philip that Hawthorne had in mind.

"Sir Philip liked the idea and said we could discuss it later that night at his new house in Hampstead. He would leave open a French door at the side of the house. I went, we talked, and I gave him as much as I had written. Interestingly, he returned the title page to me—'No names,' he said—and, squaring all the pages, laid the manuscript on his desk. Then I left."

"So," charged Holmes, "you do now admit that you were at the scene of the murder on the night of the crime."

"Yes, but, believe me, Sir Philip was very much alive when I left."

"You were in the library then?"

"Yes."

"Did you see the knife used in the killing?"

"I saw a long package, but I didn't know that it was a knife—at least, not then."

"Why didn't you tell all this to the police—or, at least, to Watson and me?"

"And put myself at the scene of a murder?" Hawthorne shook his head. "I already confessed that I have financial problems; I don't need to add the charge of murder to my list."

We now knew of at least three suspects who had appeared at Ghent House the night of Sir Philip's murder—not to mention any other of Sir Philip's enemies like Jaco van Rooyen, the disgruntled member of the Pericles Club about whom we had heard from the doorman. Two had been identified—the already-convicted Lovelace, of course, and now the impecunious Julian Hawthorne. There remained at least one more unknown personage—or so we had been led to believe by the housekeeper, Mrs. Charles—the slight, bearded fellow of whom she had a hazy memory as he conversed with Sir Philip in the library late into the night.

Holmes thanked Hawthorne for his candour and told him we would keep him abreast of any new developments which he could then pass along to Lovelace.

The American forced himself to stand and headed for the door.

Though he did not appear to have the energy to say anything else, Holmes did. "One final word before you leave, Hawthorne," he cautioned. "Keep Lovelace away from the police."

Chapter Eleven

Resolution

The assumption that a criminal class
exists among us separate and distinct
from any and the best of the rest of us
is Pharisaical, false, and wicked.
--Julian Hawthorne
The Subterranean
Brotherhood (1914)

Wednesday morning brought us a surprise. Billy the page entered to announce the arrival of Mrs. Elizabeth Perle, Mercédès' elderly mother.

"Sweet old thing, she is," Billy advised us before she came in, "but terribly upset. She wants to speak to *you*, Dr. Watson."

"To *me*?" I asked, "not to Mr Holmes?" But then I remembered that Mrs. Perle and I had met in her flat on Sunday and that she had never encountered my friend. "Show her in, Billy," I said.

The lad's description fit Mrs. Perle perfectly. In spite of a knit scarf that covered her grey hair and a long wool coat wrapped about her, she still shivered as she approached me.

"Pray, tell us what is the matter, Mrs. Perle," I said. "It isn't cold enough to warrant your condition." I indicated a nearby wingchair.

But Mrs. Perle did not move. "Mercédès is missing," she said simply. "You seemed to know much about the matter when you visited us with Mr. Hawthorne the other day. That's why I came here now." She took both of my hands in hers. "Find my daughter, Dr. Watson."

I introduced her to Holmes and explained how he was the detective in charge. But before Holmes could say a word, Billy returned, this time with a telegram, which he handed to Holmes before exiting.

My friend read it quickly, then passed it to me. Here is what I read:

To Sherlock Holmes:
If Lovelace wishes to see Mercedes again, he must sign a confession re-affirming that he murdered Sir Philip, and Dr. Watson must leave it with the publican in the Tabard Inn at 3:00 this afternoon. If you want to see Mercedes alive, you must not go to the police.

Although I was caught up with my own involvement in the plot, it was Mrs. Perle who asked the appropriate question regarding the telegram. "Is it about my daughter? She didn't come down for breakfast, you see, and she wasn't in her room. I know something has happened to her. And she seemed so happy yesterday."

Suddenly, we heard heavy footsteps on the stairs. Billy opened the door again, but before he could get out a word, Vincent Lovelace entered and brushed past the boy who now slinked out of the room.

"I went to Mercédès'—she invited me for breakfast this morning—and no one was there, not even her mother."

Holmes took the opportunity to introduce Lovelace to the older woman standing next to him.

But the artist was too heated to be cordial. "This morning I saw the carriage on the Albert Bridge again," he announced, "the one from yesterday that almost ran us down. It was travelling south, its windows were open, and it looked empty."

"You're sure it was the same?" I asked.

"Dark-green, no crests. It was the same."

"Someone could have been tied up and lying on the floor," I said.

"True, Watson," said Holmes, "but probability suggests that someone else would be sitting inside to watch over the captive." Turning towards Lovelace, Holmes handed him the telegram we had just received.

"Why can't we find these people and force them to tell us where Mercédès is?" Lovelace demanded after reading the message. "Why can't we simply watch the pub, catch whoever comes for my confession, and force them to give us the information?"

"Because, Lovelace," Holmes reminded the artist, "we're trying to save *you* as well. I'm sure you haven't forgotten that—however unfairly—not only have you been sentenced to death, but you are also a fugitive. Since most assuredly whoever took Miss Perle also knows these facts, we must tread lightly in our attempt to recover her."

"To save Mercédès," said Lovelace nobly, "I'll sign any confession the kidnapper wants. My only concern is getting her back."

"Amen," said Mrs. Perle quietly. The artist's last comment seemed all the poor woman was able to understand about the matter.

"And I'll convey the agreement to the Tabard," I said, "though I'd prefer a more positive outcome."

"Agreed," said Holmes, "but let's not be injudicious. Before you sign anything,

Lovelace, and before you give it to anyone, Watson, let's take a look at the Perles' flat and see if we might be able to discover among ourselves what happened to her."

I arranged with Mrs. Hudson to look after Mercédès' mother, but before we left our rooms, Holmes said, "Watson, be so kind as to bring along your pistol. I'm afraid we're dealing with some desperate people."

I placed my Adams revolver in a coat pocket and followed Holmes and Lovelace out onto the street. Beneath a bright blue sky, Holmes hailed a taxi, and the three of us returned to Mercédès' flat in Chelsea to see what we could learn.

Before setting foot in the building, however, Holmes walked round the premises. Only after he had examined the outer doors and scrutinised the ground, especially in the mews near the rear door, did we enter the block and locate the Perles' flat on the first floor.

The door was unlocked.

"Mrs. Perle probably left it that way in her haste to come see us," I suggested.

"Perhaps," said Holmes, but pointing to scratches about the lock, he added, "though it would appear that someone who knows how to pick a lock has been at work here."

We entered the sitting room and made our way through a corridor to a bedroom.

Thanks to the numerous frocks and gowns hanging in an armoire, the small bottles of scent posed before an oval mirror, and the yellow boater lying on a table, one could readily assume the chambre to be that of Mercédès Perle. As it turned out, however, the most significant clue to what had happened appeared to be the lack of any clues at all.

"There is no sign of a struggle," Holmes said. "Presumably, her abductor threatened her in some way. The fresh horse-droppings in the mews suggest that a carriage—probably, the green four-wheeler with which we are familiar—had been left behind the building when the crime was committed. At some time in the early hours of the morning, the poor girl had been snatched, placed in the carriage, and taken to some secret hiding place."

It all made perfect sense.

"If, as we believe," Holmes observed, "the carriage was empty when it was seen by Lovelace on the nearby bridge, we may assume that the victim was left somewhere close by. What is more, since there is no reason to believe that the kidnapper has any particular knowledge of this area, one might reasonably conclude that Miss Perle is hidden somewhere near the bridge."

The bridge, I thought. *What about the bridge?* Suddenly, I remembered Roland Wattle's quip. "An empty tollbooth!" I blurted out. "It's perfect. There are four at the Albert Bridge. I've seen them. They're unused, and the toll windows are shut. The doors are presumably locked, but probably easy for anyone with the will to get into."

"Good show, Watson!" Holmes cried. "Let's go have a look then, shall we?"

Beneath a high sun, the three of us—Holmes, Lovelace, and I—hastened down various streets and turnings until we reached the steps leading up to the Chelsea side of the Albert Bridge. I followed as best I could, my vision of joining a hiking club dissipating as I fell farther behind. In fact, by the time I caught up to them, Holmes and Lovelace had already moved from the western booth at the Chelsea end to the other booth across the road. Checking the small eastern structure made more sense, of course, since it stood next to the lane of traffic heading south—not only away from Chelsea, but also away from central London and Scotland Yard.

"Note the scratches," said Holmes pointing to the door of the tollbooth. "Another picked lock." With those words, he extricated from his coat a small packet of lock-picking tools and within a minute had the door open.

"Mercédès!" shouted Lovelace, for indeed the young woman clad in her dressing gown lay bound and gagged on the small, octagonal floor. Lovelace was at her side in an instant and removed the cloth covering her mouth.

"He had a gun," she gasped. "There were two of them. The small one had the gun. He said he would shoot my mother if I didn't go with them. I had no choice. They tied me up and brought me here."

"Let's get you home," Lovelace said, untying her bonds and draping his coat about her. "Then we can deal with the people responsible for this horror." Suddenly, he cried out, "What the deuce—?"

A figure had blocked the doorway, a slight fellow with a beard, dressed in dark coat and trousers. More to the point, he was holding a pistol—an Adams, as far as I could tell, not unlike my own army revolver. In fact, I made a move to secure the Adams in my pocket, but I was detected. The intruder put out his free hand whilst employing the other to aim the barrel of his gun between my eyes. I had no choice but to give up my pistol, the handle-end first.

Maintaining a strict eye on all of us, the villain snatched the gun from my grip, took a step backward out of the tollbooth, and tossed my gun into the Thames. Repositioning himself in the open doorway, he moved his own gun-barrel back and forth sidling us together in the confined space. It was clear that he intended to keep us out of sight to anyone passing by.

"This has to end now," he said. His voice was high-pitched, and though he seemed a stranger, there was something familiar about him. Then, to the surprise of almost everyone huddled closely next to one another, he reached up with his free hand and pulled off his beard. Fiona Plumb revealed herself. She seemed proud of her ability to have deceived us.

Clearly not deceived, Sherlock Holmes said, "You've merely corroborated the obvious. I've known from the start that you were a fraud. Your marriage certificate is a fake. You were no more married to Sir Philip Ghent than I was."

"Is it so hard to believe, Mr. Holmes," said she, her voice sounding sugary but false, "that a man like Sir Philip would not be interested in marrying a charming woman like myself? In any case, it is what that villain led me to expect."

Holmes responded with a brief laugh.

Though Fiona Plumb said nothing in response, she narrowed her bilious eyes as if to take the measure of this man who refused to be fooled by her.

"For obvious reasons," she said, waving her gun at us as she spoke, "I can't afford any of you to reveal my history. I'm sure that when a 'bus comes lumbering over the bridge, the sound of gunshots will be drowned out by the noise."

The four of us stood close together. Lovelace had his arm round Mercédès. I sensed Holmes was waiting for the right time to make a move, but I could not imagine what that move was going to be. Gambling on whether a ruthless Fiona Plumb would risk a series of gunshots without the noise to cover them seemed a very bad wager indeed.

Desperately hoping no 'bus would come into view, we watched a few growlers and hansoms pass by. Suddenly, a voice rang out from beyond the open door. "Hello, there!"

Fiona whirled about to see Julian Hawthorne, one hand shielding his eyes from the sun, the other waving in friendly fashion as he innocently approached the tollbooth.

Holmes literally jumped at the opportunity and, leaping at the woman, grabbed both of her wrists in a vise-like grip with his long fingers. She gasped in pain and dropped the pistol. I was directly behind Holmes and immediately retrieved the gun. Oh, the woman hurled a series of unladylike imprecations at us, but once Holmes had successfully subdued her, I pointed her own revolver at her to keep her in check.

"What's going on here?" Hawthorne wanted to know. "Lovelace said he was having breakfast with Mercédès and even though I had no invitation, I decided to invite myself along."

"And we're very happy that you did," Lovelace chuckled. "At least *this* time," he added, and we all breathed a sigh of relief.

"I saw the growler again," Hawthorne said. "It was parked by the bridge. That's what brought me over this way."

"The growler," Holmes repeated with alarm, but it was already too late. Fiona Plumb's man Friday, Roland Wattle, in grey wig and scarf, was approaching us, pistol drawn and aimed directly at my head.

"Put the gun down," Wattle said to me. To Holmes, he ordered, "Let her go."

Fiona Plumb wrenched herself free as I placed the pistol on the floor. She picked up the gun and moved next to her henchman.

"Good work," she said, joining Wattle in pointing a gun at all of us. "Now we wait for something heavy to rumble past, and then we finish our task."

Moments earlier, we thought we had been saved. Now it seemed that we had but a short time to live, especially when after a minute or two a large omnibus appeared in the distance at the Battersea end of the bridge. It was packed with passengers and had four large draught horses pulling it instead of the usual two. Given the distance it needed to reach us, I realised that we had only a few moments left.

"Ready?" Fiona said to Wattle.

"Right," he answered.

It was just then that "The Trembling Lady" lived up to her nickname. Though the tollbooth we occupied was at the far end of the roadway, the pounding of the horses' hooves and the lumbering of the heavy 'bus as it approached us over the full length of the bridge amplified the rolling effect— amplified it enough at least to throw our captors off balance.

In an instant, Holmes once more leapt at Fiona and, as before, constricted her wrists in his tenacious grasp. Only after the gun fell out of her useless hand and clattered on the floor did he release his hold.

In the same moment, Hawthorne catapulted himself at Wattle's chest, using his hands to thrust the gunman's arms upward. The pistol discharged, the explosive report reverberating within the restrictive confines of the tollbooth. But the bullet struck only the ceiling and Wattle, falling backwards, struck his head on the doorjamb before hitting the floor. Hawthorne attacked with speed and dexterity, sending a vicious kick to Wattle's gun-hand before setting himself on the villain's prone body and rendering him immobile. As for the pistol, it skidded on its side through the open door and out onto the walkway.

To our great relief, the entire struggle was over in seconds. Fiona and Wattle may have been killers, but fighters they were not, and Holmes and Hawthorne had them under control.

"Good work," Holmes said to the American as he collected both of the guns that only moments before had been threatening us.

"I used to be a gymnast at Harvard, you know," Hawthorne smiled.

"Glad to see your education at work," said Holmes wryly. "Now, Hawthorne, be so kind as to take us to where you spied the growler."

"I'll see Mercédès home," Lovelace announced and guided the young woman in the direction of her flat. At the same time, Hawthorne and Holmes led our captives towards the green four-wheeler.

As I soon discovered, Holmes counted driving a carriage among his many talents, and with the crack of his whip, we set out for Scotland Yard. Inside the four-wheeler, Hawthorne and I kept pistols trained on our prisoners.

As chance would have it, the detective who joined us at the carriage-entrance to Scotland Yard a half-hour later turned out to be the tall and fair-haired Inspector Gregson, the same Tobias Gregson whose case history served as the plot for Julian Hawthorne's ill-fated crime story.

"Always good to see you, Mr. Holmes," Gregson greeted my friend. "You too, Dr. Watson. And Mr. Hawthorne here too? Still no royalties for me, I presume."

Hawthorne merely shook his head.

Finally, Gregson turned his attention to the two figures we held under guard. "What have we here?" he said, walking up to the pair and looking Fiona Plumb and Roland Wattle up and down.

Holmes informed him of all that had come to pass, and with a quick nod, Gregson proceeded to march our prisoners off to be processed.

The familiar Inspector Lestrade greeted us inside the building where it would fall upon him to write a comprehensive report of not only what had just occurred to us on the bridge, but also the new information Holmes would provide related to the years-old killing in Ghent House.

A sentimentalist might note—might even call it fitting—that Gregson and Lestrade, the pair of police rivals I depicted in *A Study in Scarlet*, played harmonious roles in concluding the arrests of the two villains. There seemed a kind of poetic justice in the entire affair.

Chapter Twelve

Dénouement

Let us recall happier things!
              --Julian Hawthorne
              The Memoirs of
              Julian Hawthorne

Sherlock Holmes spent the late hours of Tuesday night furnishing Inspector Lestrade with the details of our investigation. Those details—along with the confessions of Fiona Plumb and Roland Wattle elicited by Gregson—constituted the basis for Lestrade's official account to be delivered to his senior officers.

Wednesday afternoon, exactly one week to the day since Hawthorne's wallet had been stolen, Holmes presented the salient features of Lestrade's report to the principals in the drama—Julian Hawthorne and the newly betrothed couple, Lovelace and Mercédès—all of whom, along with Mrs. Perle, had joined us for sherry in our Baker Street sitting room.

"Fiona Plumb," Holmes began, "was an ambitious actress whose beauty and talent attracted the wealthy Sir Philip Ghent. In search of money and power, she assumed—incorrectly, as it turned out—that Sir Philip intended to marry her and, as a result, that all his riches would someday be hers.

"When Sir Philip told Fiona of his desire to wed his distant cousin Mercédès Perle, however, he ignited a resentment in Fiona that would lead to his death."

"'Hell hath no fury . . . ,'" quoted Hawthorne, raising his sherry.

"Sir Philip," Holmes continued, "made the mistake of telling Fiona that he planned to dine at his club the night in question and then sleep for the first time in his new house in Hampstead. Those words turned out to be all the scheming Fiona needed to hear. She outfitted herself as the bearded fellow observed by the doorman and later by the housekeeper—"

"Hold on," I said. "Didn't she boast about playing Rosalind in *As You Like It*, a woman who poses as a man?"

"Quite so," said Holmes. "In just such a disguise, she waited outside the Pericles and proceeded to follow Sir Philip all the way to Ghent House. Once having arrived, she concealed herself outside the dining room by an open French window—"

"That's the side-door entrance where Sir Philip told *me* to meet him," said Hawthorne.

"Right," agreed Holmes. "In fact, Hawthorne, you were there when she got to the house, and she planned on waiting until you completed your business with Sir Philip concerning your Gregson-story before she made her move. But no sooner did *you* leave than Lovelace knocked on the front door and was admitted by Mrs. Charles. Still outside at the nearby French window, Fiona grew angry all over again as she overheard the row between Lovelace and Sir Philip related to your guardian's intention to marry you, Miss Perle."

Mercédès shook her head.

"Once Lovelace exited, Fiona, pistol in hand, quietly entered the house through the open French window. It was when she walked into the adjacent library that she discovered Sir Philip had already unwrapped the package on his desk containing Lovelace's Japanese knife."

"Actually," said Lovelace, "I unwrapped it myself."

"What luck!" exclaimed Hawthorne, his voice exuding sarcasm.

"Lucky for *her*," Holmes said, "although one does not like to think that Dame Fortune smiles on such murderous evil-doers. Nonetheless, Fiona arrived just as Sir Philip was opening his safe—"

"To keep my crime story in a secure place," Hawthorne reminded everyone.

"Indeed," said Holmes with a note of irritation. Yet truth be told, by then we all were growing accustomed to Hawthorne's interruptions.

"Despite her disguise," Holmes continued, "Sir Philip recognised Fiona, and they argued across the desk—where Mrs. Charles espied them. Minutes later, when Sir Philip stood up and turned away from her, Fiona, avoiding the sound of gunshots, grabbed the knife and plunged it into his back."

"The poor man," murmured Mercédès.

"It was quiet in the house, and Fiona took the opportunity to search through all the papers in the safe. That was when she found the will that left Sir Philip's estate, including Ghent House, to you, Miss Perle."

"I still can't believe it," whispered Mercédès.

"Fiona took the document and paid a forger to copy it quickly but to insert her own name in the place of Mercédès Perle's. To make the business seem legitimate, she also had the forger create the fraudulent marriage certificate. To complete the subterfuge, she posed as a maid at the Pericles and managed to place the newly forged documents in Sir Philip's desk."

"Almost a perfect crime," I observed.

"As she believed herself," said Holmes, "until she heard that the so-called murderer had returned to England. She told Gregson that she never believed that you were killed in the 'bus collision, Lovelace, and she hired lookouts to watch the train stations and the docks for days after the crash to see if you re-appeared. Once she learned you had got to Germany, she felt safe again—as long as you stayed there."

"Three years," Lovelace reminded everyone.

"Even so, with her inherited fortune, she had the money to pay people in Dresden to keep an eye on you, and she had you trailed from Dover after you arrived back in England. When you followed Hawthorne to Harrods, *you* were followed as well, and once you attempted to speak to Hawthorne at the jewellery counter, Wattle, in disguise—"

"The grey-haired man with the cane," recalled Hawthorne.

"Quite so," agreed Holmes. "Wattle tried to falsely incriminate you for stealing Hawthorne's wallet. Once you were arrested, you see, Fiona Plumb trusted that the police would discover your true identity and you'd be sent back to prison and hanged."

Lovelace shook his head.

"But Wattle ruined the plan. He became greedy and kept all the banknotes in the wallet for himself."

"Ha!" laughed Hawthorne. "No honour among thieves."

"Good that you can laugh about it," said Holmes. "It seems he spent all your money, including those greenbacks."

Hawthorne's smile disappeared immediately.

"After that scheme failed," Holmes continued, "Fiona reckoned—correctly, as it turned out—that you, Lovelace, would come back to see Miss Perle. Keeping an eye on the Chelsea flat, she used Miss Perle as bait. In a word, she planned to kill you—all of you, really—to continue her life as Lady Ghent."

"What about Wattle?" asked Hawthorne.

"A fellow actor," said Holmes, "though equally unsuccessful on the stage— But eager to do Fiona's bidding once she told him how much she would be paying him."

"A woman like that?" Hawthorne sneered. "I imagine she offered him more than just money. Something more, more intimate—maybe even marriage."

"Actually, Hawthorne," Holmes said, "you bring Wattle up at just the right moment, for it was Wattle we have to thank for preserving the original will. He told Gregson how he managed to grab it from the fire after Fiona had thrown it in and left the room. Wattle planned to use the real will as insurance should Fiona ever turn against him. To that end, he had taped the slightly-burned pages to the underside of a drawer in his room in Ghent House. It was Gregson who found them."

"I knew he was a good copper," said Hawthorne.

Holmes sipped his sherry, then said, "I should add that it was the grey-wigged Wattle, face covered with the plaid scarf, who tried to run down the two of you on the Albert Bridge."

Mercédès and Lovelace clutched each other's hand. Mrs. Perle simply shook her head.

"Now that Fiona and Wattle have been arrested," Hawthorne asked, "what, pray tell, is to be the fate of my friend Lovelace?"

"Lestrade has assured me," said Holmes, "that the original murder charge against Vincent Louder Lovelace will be withdrawn and that without any doubt a judge will agree."

The artist smiled broadly, and Mercédès kissed his cheek.

That Hawthorne had asked the question about the resolution of the case against Lovelace reflected the American's keen interest all the while Holmes had been speaking. Whilst Hawthorne had no notebook in hand, his attentiveness to detail and plot suggested the obvious—that as he absorbed Holmes's account, he was already formulating the intricacies of a novel of his own.

Julian Hawthorne had previously admitted that he was constantly seeking markets for his written work. Though the anonymous manuscript found in Sir Philip's safe never interested any publishers, one could count on the fact that Hawthorne was not the sort of literary entrepreneur whose efforts to provide an income with his pen could easily be thwarted.

Chapter Thirteen

Literary Considerations

. . .This book was not designed
to be a record of facts, but of facts
as regenerated and purified by memory.
--Julian Hawthorne
Shapes that Pass

Years later, I would read that upon
Hawthorne's return to the United States in
March of '82, he did, as he had told us he
would, make arrangements with the New
York Chief of Detectives, Thomas Byrnes,
for access to the department's files. Known
affectionately as Byrnes' "Literary Pard"—
that is, "literary partner" (or so Holmes
assured me)—Hawthorne has thus far
produced five novels based on the stories he
mined from Byrnes' experiences.[6]

---

[6] The number remained at five: *The Great Bank
Robbery* (1887), *An American Penman* (1887), *A
Tragic Mystery* (1887), *Section 558* (1888), and
Another's Crime (1888).

As for Julian Hawthorne's interpretation of the fall and rise of artist Vincent Louder Lovelace, I correctly recognised that, just as with the files of Inspector Byrnes, commercial interests would dictate Hawthorne's approach. Employing the literary adroitness he inherited from his distinguished father, Julian romanticised the frightful details of the factual Ghent murder.

In his popular version, the ever-melodramatic Julian not only changed names and set the English investigation in America, but he also added divergent subplots featuring mysterious necromancers and trance-inducing spiritualists. Nor was sensationalism beyond him. Leaving nothing to the imagination, Hawthorne offered no hesitancy in describing such details as the contours of a woman's figure in diaphanous clothing.

At the same time, he clearly recognised the need to stage his fantasy in a framework of reality. Thus, he invoked a variety of allusions to historical events. The Battle of Sedan that resulted in Germany's victory in the Franco-Prussian War played a role in his novel as did references to actual figures like the emperor Louis-Napoleon, generals Bazaine and MacMahon, and the banking family of the Rothschilds.

It should also come as little surprise that in order to popularise his re-imagining of Lovelace's story, the profit-minded Hawthorne turned to Dumas' highly successful tale of Edmond Dantès. One recalls that on a number of occasions during the actual investigation, the American actually cited the perilous adventures of Dantès and his resurrection.[7]

Whilst it may simply have been the name, Mercédès, that served as catalyst, in all probability that which most attracted Hawthorne to Dumas' story was the parallels between the falsely reported death of the very real Vincent Lovelace—thought to have died in the collision with the 'bus—and the metaphorical death of the fictional Edmond Dantès—condemned to an unjust life's-sentence in the dungeons of *Chateau d'If* (as Hawthorne had reminded me).

---

[7] As noted earlier, Dumas's novel is itself reputed to be a reconstruction of an actual criminal case. According to Luc Sante in the Barnes & Noble introduction to *The Count of Monte Cristo*, Dumas found the story of a young shoemaker who was falsely accused of a crime by three associates and imprisoned for seven years. Upon his release, he sought revenge, murdering (among others) the men responsible for lying about him and labeling their corpses, Numbers One, Two, and Three.

Cloaking his fictional representation of Lovelace in the persona of a common artist called Keppel Darke who metamorphosises into the wealthy Count Lucien de Lisle, Hawthorne mirrored Dumas' reincarnation of Edmond Dantès. For after escaping his imprisonment, Dantès recovers a treasure and emerges as a wealthy count. It must be remembered, however, that though both Dumas' and Hawthorne's fictional characters return from the dead with fabulous fortunes, in reality, Lovelace himself had only limited financial resources.

In the end, if any doubts concerning Hawthorne's indebtedness to Dumas still remain, they will inevitably be erased by the title of Hawthorne's fictional rendering of the case through which Holmes and I had just navigated: *An American Monte Cristo.*

One can only wonder if in 1913, when American authorities jailed Julian Hawthorne for fraud, he discerned similarities between his own fate and that of the falsely-imprisoned Edmond Dantès. Like Dantès, Hawthorne blamed his troubles on the duplicity of his so-called friends, but at least the American author, lacking the wealth of Dumas' Count, did not devote the rest of his life to seeking revenge.

An American Monte Cristo sold well,[8] especially in England, yet Julian would admit in his later years that of the thirty novels and novellas he had written, there were perhaps only half a dozen of which he was not ashamed. As far as either Holmes or I can attest, he has yet to identify any of them.

Hawthorne and his family moved to Jamaica at the end of '94 where he hoped to make his fortune as a farmer. Though as anyone who has met the mercurial author could have predicted, he did not succeed in this venture, he did at least find in Jamaica a setting for the feeble plot of "The Adventure of the Lost Object," his 1895 parody of one of my own sketches about Sherlock Holmes.[9]

Although it is said that imitation is the sincerest form of flattery, there seems little of complimentary value in Hawthorne's depiction of Holmes and me. In addition to his misguided attempt to replicate my

---

[8] In *Hawthorne's Son: The Life and Literary Career of Julian Hawthorne*, Maurice Bassan refers to the novel as "glittering rubbish" but adds "that at least it paid some of Hawthorne's bills."

[9] "The Adventure of the Lost Object" was syndicated in April 1895, appearing in the *Nashville Banner* (16 April), *Worcester Spy* (17 April), *Louisville Courier-Journal* (21 April), and *Winnipeg Tribune* (22 April).

narrative voice, Hawthorne portrayed the two of us as covert salesmen who encourage readers to "procure" my published volumes of Holmes's adventures at bookshops, "price $1.25."

Worse, he exaggerated to the point of ridicule Holmes's keen skill in extracting information from the most minute of clues. Hawthorne's Holmes (wrongly) declares a lost knife to be found in the gullet of a buzzard that ate a dead dog that swallowed the knife that fell from a pocket, the original error which inadvertently enables the knife to be found.

Some might think it clever, yet I regard the story as caustic and mean-spirited. In light of how we had worked to exonerate Hawthorne's friend Lovelace, the fact that neither Holmes nor I could discover anything of a positive nature in the piece continues to mystify. . . .

Epilogue

Only an artist can make a permanent
contribution to human civilization,
for his work is born of the spirit, and is unique
. . . . [A work] by a master of art will revive and
instruct us forever.
                                    --Julian Hawthorne
                                    Shapes that Pass

Despite his constant complaints about
being underpaid for his writings, in the years
following the solution to the Ghent murder
case, Julian Hawthorne figured prominently
as a popular author.   To Holmes and me,
however, his name appeared but sporadically.

One example pertains to an influential
meeting of literati held at the Langham Hotel
on 30 August, 1889. As I was informed by
Conan Doyle who was in attendance, Joseph
Stoddart, the managing editor of the
American magazine, *Lippincott's Monthly,*
hoped to promote a British edition of the
American periodical.

Stoddart, who also happened to be
Hawthorne's friend and literary agent,
mentioned the author in seeking

contributions to the new publication from the pair of distinguished attendees—Conan Doyle, who labelled the event a "golden evening," and Oscar Wilde, who at the time was known primarily for his poetry and essays. Stoddart cited the sales of Hawthorne's novella, *Sinfire*, a sensational tale of love and murder, for which three years before, *Lippincott's* paid the author $1000.

Apparently, evoking the success of Julian Hawthorne served its purpose. Not only did *Sinfire* demonstrate *Lippincott's* popular appeal, but it also represented the magazine's generosity in rewarding its writers. Wilde responded with the novel, *The Picture of Dorian Gray*, whilst Conan Doyle submitted *The Sign of Four*, my personal narrative concerning Sherlock Holmes and the theft of the Agra treasure.[10]

Periodically, we would also encounter Hawthorne's name in the newspapers. Earlier during that same month of August in '89, it was reported that Hawthorne himself had returned to London as part of a Continental tour observing European workers. And eight years later, in

---

[10] Watson modestly refrains from mentioning that his account also reports the introduction of his future wife, Miss Mary Morstan.

February of '97, I read that he had arrived in London as a reporter for *Cosmopolitan* magazine en route to the South Asian subcontinent to write of starvation in India.

Yet in spite of the relationship which Holmes and I shared with Julian Hawthorne in resolving the fate of Vincent Louder Lovelace—not to mention the emotional confessions some of us were forced to make along the way—Hawthorne clearly saw little reason to contact Holmes or me upon returning to England.

Perhaps, he saw no commercial advantage in such a meeting; perhaps, he foresaw little chance in such a visit resulting in an encounter with a *femme fatale*. Whatever the man's thinking, scrutiny of his schedule will reveal that on neither occasion upon reappearing in London did the unpredictable scion of Nathaniel Hawthorne deign to make an appearance in Baker Street.

THE END

Editor's Notes

Readers interested in Julian Hawthorne's accounts of the major events in Watson's narrative are referred to two of Hawthorne's novels in particular, *An American Monte Cristo* and *Another's Crime: From the Diary of Inspector Byrnes*.   Interestingly, both novels deal with men who, like Vincent Lovelace, take on false identities.   In addition, the latter work portrays a relationship between an older man and a much younger woman like the proposed marriage of Sir Philip and Mercédès in Watson's narrative.

Two biographies review the life of Julian Hawthorne. Maurice Bassan's *Hawthorne's Son: The Life and Literary Career of Julian Hawthorne* (published in 1970) and Gary Scharnhorst's *Julian Hawthorne: The Life of a Prodigal Son* (2014). The more recent study benefits from later scholarship in areas like Julian Hawthorne's previously unknown second (and secret) family with Minna Desborough, whose children were only acknowledged in the public reading of

Hawthorne's will in 1910. It should also be pointed out that, consistent with Watson's observations at the end of his narrative, neither Bassan nor Scharnhorst makes any mention of Julian Hawthorne's efforts to meet with Holmes and Watson in the years following the resolution of Philip Ghent's murder.

For an extended discussion of the relationship between Julian Hawthorne and Inspector Thomas Byrnes, see *The Origins of the American Detective Story* by LeRoy Lad Panek.

For the adventurous reader, Dumas' *The Count of Monte Cristo* beckons. There are numerous editions and translations of the epic novel as well as a large number of movies that attempt to tell the tale. Silent film versions appeared during Julian Hawthorne's lifetime, one of which starred James O'Neill, the father of playwright Eugene O'Neill. The senior O'Neill based his cinematic interpretation of Edmond Dantès on that of his stage performances depicting the character, a highly remunerative role which he perpetuated for decades.

The celebrated film featuring Robert Donat appeared in 1934, the same year as Julian Hawthorne's death. Other popular film versions were made in 1975 and 2002. In 2024, ninety years after Donat's film (and almost 180 years since the publication of the novel itself), a successful French version was produced, confirming the lasting appeal of Dumas' story.